EMBATTLED SEAL

BY
J.M. MADDEN

If you would like to read about the 'combat modified'
veterans of the **Lost and Found Investigative Service**,
check out these books:

The Embattled Road (FREE prequel)
Embattled Hearts – Book 1
Embattled Minds – Book 2
Embattled Home – Book 3
Her Forever Hero – Grif
SEAL's Lost Dream – Flynn
Unbreakable SEAL – Max

OTHER BOOKS BY J.M. MADDEN

A Touch of Fae
Second Time Around
A Needful Heart
Wet Dream
Love on the Line Book 1
Love on the Line Book 2
The Awakening Society – FREE
Tempt Me
Urban Moon Anthology

If you'd like to connect with me on social media and keep updated on my releases, try these links:

Newsletter: jmmadden.com/newsletter.htm
Website: jmmadden.com
Facebook: facebook.com/jmmaddenauthor
Twitter: @authorjmmadden
Tsū: www.tsu.co/JMMadden

And of course you can always email me at authorjmmadden@gmail.com

ACKNOWLEDGEMENTS

As always I have to thank my husband. If it wasn't for your never-ending support I could never have realized my dream. Love you, Babe!

Donna and Robyn, you girls are simply amazing! You have the best advice. Thank you for reminding me to stick with my gut.

To the Madden Militia, you ladies rock! Sandie, Mayas, Mary, Elizabeth, Andrea, Mistie, Karen — thank you all for your input!

DEDICATION

I had the pleasure of attending a meeting last year with retired US Navy SEAL Don Shipley and his wife Diane, as well as an amazing group of fellow military writers. As incredible as Don was, I remember being incredibly impressed with Diane. She loved her husband but she had an iron hard will that I've only ever seen in single mothers and other military wives.

This is for all the servicemen and their families, especially the women (and sometimes men) that keep everything together at home. I know it's not an easy life and I admire every one of you that manages to make a life centered around the military.

Thank you!

CHAPTER ONE

FIVE MILLION THOUGHTS raced through her head as Cat shoved her way through a group of men and into the hospital room. She had no idea who the men were, only that they were keeping her from her husband.

As she stepped to the side of the bed and took in everything attached to him and in him, she wanted to rail at the world. This wasn't how she wanted to reconnect with Harper. This wasn't how it was supposed to play out. Damn it. She wanted to jerk him up and hold him against her, make him open his beautiful storm-cloud silver eyes and tell her he loved her.

But he hadn't done that for a long time.

Her eyes catalogued the machines. He was on a ventilator; saline dripped steadily into his arm along with another clear fluid she couldn't see the sticker of. Probably some kind of pain med or antibiotic.

There was a deep scuff on his heavy jaw and dark hair had already begun to shadow his cheeks, but the top of his head was swathed with bandages. Both eyes were completely covered and her stomach bottomed out at the worry that caused. They'd left the johnny hospital gown hanging untied, merely draped over his massive chest. They probably couldn't have tied it even if he'd been vertical. Her husband was usually too big for one-size-fits-all.

Lifting the edge of the fabric, she found several heavy-duty bandages high on his chest. What the hell had happened? She looked at the men still standing at the door, staring at her now as if she were crazy. "Are one of you a doctor? Tell me what happened."

All three of them moved to the end of the bed, watching her. But the one with the slender black cane spoke up. "I'm Preston's employer, Duncan Wilde. Would you explain who you are, please?"

Cat looked the man up and down. Forties, salt and pepper hair, a little grayer on the sides. Kind, experienced brown eyes. "I'm his wife, Cat. Estranged for the past year and a half, but still his wife. Why didn't you call me if you're his employer?"

The man shifted against his black cane, his gaze going to the man on the opposite end of the trio. "Honestly, there was no beneficiary contact in his employment file. Who *did* call you?"

Cat blinked. "I think the hospital. The VA, I mean. Not this one."

The gray haired man with glasses spoke up. "I called the local VA to let them know he had been injured and to get his medical records. They must have called her." He stepped forward, hand outstretched. "Dr. Reynolds. I just operated on your...husband. He's had significant damage..."

Cat struggled to focus as the doctor went through the list of major and minor injuries, but her eyes kept drifting back to Harper's form on the bed. He seemed bulkier to her, even lying the way he was. But his face seemed leaner. Deep grooves bracketed his broad mouth and her fingers itched to stroke them away. Damn, after eighteen months she should have been pissed and in the back of her mind she knew she was, but she was happier to see him right now. Thrilled, actually. If she could crawl into the bed and lay on top of him without hurting him further she would do it.

The doctor was still going on, cautioning her about getting her hopes up. She laughed and shook her head at the man. "You have no idea what—or who—you're talking about. Harper will be fine. He's been shot before. Several times. He's been blown up, his foot has been run over, his right leg shattered. Three years ago he went into Afghanistan to rescue a helicopter crew that had gone down and his team got hit pretty bad."

He looked at her askance but she'd seen the look before. From other doctors and other injuries. Her husband had the constitution of a bull and she wouldn't let anybody plant seeds of doubt in her heart.

"Why are his eyes bandaged?" she asked, needing the conversation to get moving.

The doctor blinked. "There is significant damage to his right eye. We removed several glass shards from the exterior but one got deep enough to damage the retina. We had a specialist come in but we're not sure if his vision can be saved."

Cat clenched her jaw and cursed. God. Why couldn't it have been his less dominant left eye? The right would be a crushing blow.

He wouldn't lose the vision. He wouldn't.

The doctor's voice faded away. "I'm sorry, ma'am."

She didn't even look up as the doctor left. Folding her arms beneath her breasts she moved closer to Harper's head and reached out to run her hand across his collarbone, then the swell of his deltoid. Her fingers relished the feel of his smooth skin after going without for so long. It felt so warm. She glanced down his arms at the tattoos, memorizing the old and new lines.

The other two men still stood against the far wall. When she looked up the younger guy gave her a compassionate smile that crinkled the skin around his bright blue eyes. "I'm sorry you walked into this blind. We really didn't know to contact you."

Cat sighed, knowing he was telling the truth. "I believe you. The only way you would have found out was if you had been in his apartment where he keeps his personal papers. Harper has tried to distance himself from us as much as possible but he still keeps our interests at heart and protected."

The men glanced at each other, frowning, as if silently asking the other if they had been in Harper's apartment. She had a feeling neither man had been. Harper's space was sacrosanct to him. Just like his weapon.

"Wait," the man with the cane said slowly. "Us?"

Cat nodded. "Harper and I have two children together, a boy and a girl. They stayed in Virginia till I could figure out what was going on."

The two men shared a dumbfounded look. Her gaze drifted back down to the bed and tears burned her eyes, but she blinked them away. He would be pissed as hell if he knew she was crying over him.

The younger guy stepped closer and held his hand out. "Chad Lowell, one of Harper's bosses. He was actually on the operation with me when he was shot."

Cat shook his hand and let go. "Can you tell me what happened?"

Nodding, Chad looked down at her husband. "We were protecting a woman and child deeper in Texas, on my family's place. Harper was up on a lookout and gave warning when the suspect showed up, but I think somebody got the drop on him. The gunshot wound to his chest was at fairly close range. We're not sure about the second. His rifle is chewed up pretty bad. We got him flown out of there as soon as possible and we were close enough to this trauma center that I think it saved his life. His warning gave us time to get the woman and child out of the house." He paused and smiled gently. "He helped us save them."

Cat swallowed, making her dry throat work. At least that had worked out. "Good. He'll be glad to know that."

The guy pulled a teddy bear from somewhere and held it out to her. "Mercy, the little girl, wanted him to have this. She said he needed it right now more than she did. But she wants it back."

She smiled as she took the raggedy old bear. Looked like it had been around the kid block a few times. She set it on the rolling bedside table so he could see it when he woke up.

She caught her breath. Damn. She'd forgotten already.

"If you don't mind, we'd like to stick around for a while," Duncan told her. "The doctor isn't sure when exactly he'll wake up."

A shiver coursed through her and she hoped that he would actually do that, then she castigated herself. Of course he was going to wake up. "That's fine. He may not be happy I'm here, so it's probably best you stay. I might have to leave."

Chad frowned but didn't pry. Cat knew he was probably burning with curiosity but he merely stepped back. "Duncan and I will be in the waiting room if you need us."

She gave a nod and watched as they left the room. Duncan, the boss, seemed to have a lot of pain to deal with. And she'd seen Chad's deformed arm.

Harper jerked heavily, as if startled, drawing her attention. But that was all he did. Perching on the edge of the guest chair she drew her phone from her pocket to send off a text message to her mother to let her know she'd arrived. She would wait as long as it would take.

SPICY LAVENDER TEASED at his consciousness, reminding him of the scent Cat used to wear. It was succulent and sexy and suited her personality to perfection. God, he missed her. Missed her steady calm-headedness in the face of all his drama. She never batted an eye at anything he did, but she would smile gently and make some remark that would center him. She understood his craziness and never got rattled.

Damn, his body hurt. What the hell had he done to himself? The flash of a muzzle from the corner of his eye made him jerk, sending furious pain slamming through his guts. Fuck, he felt like he'd had the shit kicked out of him.

No, he'd been shot. Images tumbled through his mind with sudden vicious clarity. He'd been on his belly in the rain and seen the glint of metal from a vehicle coming up the drive. He'd barely made contact with Chad on the radio when his amazingly sharp sixth sense that had saved him so many times before made him shift and turn his head. The gun that had been aimed at him from the back had fired, slamming through his chest. He'd lain there for a heartbeat of time waiting to see if it was a fatal wound, but movement had drawn his gaze. The shooter was taking off, obviously thinking the job had been completed. Forcing his limbs to move, Harper swung his weapon around and brought it up to take aim when the second shot struck. But it didn't hit him. It hit his weapon and scope. Instinctively he slammed his eyes shut, but the damage was already done. Agony tore through his face and he knew his ticket had been punched. The mercenary was getting away and he couldn't do anything about it. At the rate he was bleeding he would be dead before anybody ever found him.

A flash of the little girl he'd been protecting crowded

out thoughts of his own pain and he hoped to high hell that she'd gotten away. That little one was too precious. She didn't deserve to be hunted that way.

Time drifted away for a while and when he roused again, pain and discomfort made him shift against the ground. Or was it a bed? It was too soft to be the ground. Focusing, he tried to open his eyes but nothing happened. He tried to raise a hand to feel the ground for his weapon but he couldn't even do that much. Anxiety began to creep in. As he shifted again just to gauge his range of motion his stomach bottomed out. He couldn't do anything.

The rhythmic swooshing sound to his right gave him some hint of where he was and an excuse for the fullness he felt in his throat. Ventilator. Fuck. It had been a few years since he'd been on one but the feeling of choking on the air being forced into his lungs came back to him in a rush and that fear gave him the strength to raise his hands to reach for the damn thing.

"Don't, Harper. I'll call for a nurse. Don't pull it out."

His movements stalled as the low, soothing voice came to his ears, shocking him into stillness. Cat?

"Harper, do you hear me?"

He gave the slightest nod of his sore head, mute, shocked that she'd cared enough to come. Emotion rolled through him and he tried to force his eyes open but something obscured his vision. He tried to lift his arms again but weakness dragged at his body. Cat leaned over him and he felt her breath brush his right ear. "Just stay still, Harper, and we'll explain everything. The nurse is here now and we'll try to get this tube out of your throat."

Every protective instinct he had urged him to get up off the bed and snatch up his weapon to control the area, but he couldn't even lift his hand. This was such a clusterfuck.

Cat was here, though. Cat would take care of everything. She would guard his back.

A different woman's voice came to him from the opposite side of the hospital bed, urging him to relax. Honestly, he tried, but when she moved slower than molasses he began to go insane. Panic began to eat at his control and he clutched the edge of the mattress. The nurse unstrapped the mouthpiece from around his head and he could contain himself no longer. Knocking her hand away, he ripped the tube from his throat and threw it aside.

Cat yelled out to try to stop him but he was beyond her calming influence. As he gagged and rolled to his side to cough, he got a sense of how much he'd just fucked up. The pain radiating through his gut from the coughing made the nausea roll and he started to retch. Unfortunately, or maybe fortunately, there was nothing in his stomach to puke up, so he just heaved in pain. That heaving made his eyes throb, sending agony through his head. For a solid three minutes he was in the purest hell he could ever imagine.

Cat cradled him to her, making sure he didn't roll completely out of the bed and rubbed her hand across his back. When his spasms began to ease, she wiped his face with a wet washcloth and helped him lay back on the mattress. Harper boiled with frustrated anger. He'd been hurt before, but never like this.

"What the hell happened?"

He barely recognized his own voice it was so rough and frail, but Cat understood him. "You were shot in the chest several days ago. You've been in to surgery a couple times since you've been here, but you are improving."

He moved his hand toward his head and she clasped his palm with her own. "You have bandages around your head because the second shot hit your weapon. You had glass in your eyes from the scope being shattered."

The breath stalled in his aching lungs and he waited for her to continue. When she didn't, he connected the dots. "My vision is gone."

"No," she sighed. "They're not sure. They won't be sure until they take the bandages off in a couple days."

Harper didn't know if he believed her or not. He was laid up, damn near as injured as he'd ever been. Would she tell him the truth right now? Maybe, maybe not.

Fuck. What the hell was a sniper supposed to do with no vision?

"Listen to me, Harper. Your right eye was the most damaged, but they think they can repair it. As much as it will drive you nuts you need to just stay calm and wait it out. It may not be as bad as we imagine."

He swallowed heavily, struggling to get his raw throat to move. Cat seemed to sense he was having issues, because he felt her swing away and come back, then a straw rested at his lips. "Go slowly. Don't want you to get sick again."

The first wash of lukewarm water down his throat felt stupid good. The second even better. It didn't feel so good when it hit his stomach though. He turned his head away as his stomach contracted again but he breathed through the nausea.

Tiredness washed over him, making his limbs feel leaden. There were so many issues he needed to deal with, but his mind was foggy. He needed to let everything go and sleep. "Think I may take a nap," he mumbled.

Cat stroked a hand down his arm and his body soaked in the attention. "You do that, Harper."

"Will you stay?"

He held his breath as he waited for her answer.

"I will," she whispered. "I would never leave you at a time like this. You know that."

Yes, he did. He let the darkness pull him down.

CAT HELD ONTO Harper's arm until the tension eased from his body. Almost immediately she felt her own tension ease. God, taking care of him was like walking a knife-edge sometimes. She knew he appreciated the companionship but he did things that compromised his health all the more. What the hell was that, ripping the tube out of his throat? Stupid man.

She lifted her hand from his hot skin and moved to

the chair behind her, sinking down as her legs gave out. She'd been here two days and she was already wrung out. Pulling her phone from her pocket she sent off a quick text message to Dillon, then leaned forward to prop her head on her hands. Tiredness made her eyelids heavy, but she kept them open as long as she could just to watch Harper.

CHAPTER TWO

H ARPER CAME ALERT when he heard the door to his room hiss open, but he didn't move. He didn't know if it was friend or foe until Chad whispered, "Preston?"

The fight-or-flight panic in him eased. "Yeah," he croaked. "I'm awake."

Though he didn't normally do it he held his hand out. Chad moved around the bed to his side and clasped his hand in an iron grip. Harper may have held it a bit longer than expected too, but he didn't give himself grief over the fact.

"Dude, you scared the hell out of us. We thought you were a goner."

Harper rocked his head on the pillow. "Nah. Takes more than a couple bullets to take me out."

Chad laughed. "I remember you saying you were an iron man when we hired you, but I didn't think you were telling the truth."

Harper reached out for the bed rail. "Crank me up, boss man."

He felt Chad lean forward and fumble at the buttons, then the head of the bed began to rise. The change in elevation made his head swim, but he breathed through the dizziness. "There's good. Damn."

"Duncan's here too, but he went to the hotel to shower and lay down for a bit. He'll be back in a while. I think being in the hospital stresses him out."

Harper felt bad for putting everybody off their routines. "You don't have to be here at all."

Chad snorted. "How could I not be? You saved all of our lives."

Inwardly he cringed. "No, I didn't. I barely keyed up the mic when I got tagged."

"Fuck, Harper, that one second of sound was enough to get Lora and Mercy out of the house and up the mountain."

Relief eased through him. He hadn't known if they were alive or dead and he'd been leery of thinking about it too long. Knowing that they had made it out of there alive clarified his own situation. The thought of Mercy's bright green eyes looking up at him, full of trust and sweetness, made his throat tight. He'd do anything for that little angel. He coughed and shook his head a little. "Tell me everything."

Chad recapped the wild night, from fighting the hired mercenaries on the porch to chasing after Lora and her daughter up the mountain and seeing her kill her ex. When he got to the end Harper knew his mouth had to be open. "Lora laid him out like that?"

Chad laughed lightly. "Yup. Damn proud of her too."

He nodded. "I would be too. That's really something."

"Speaking of really something, why didn't you tell us you were married? And had kids?"

Harper cringed, knowing that the question was coming but unable to formulate an answer. "Cat and I have had some issues."

Chad didn't say anything but Harper could hear the question in the silence. He made a motion with his hand. "Not something I want to talk about, boss man."

"Okay," Chad murmured. "It's a little strange though. We're not sure what to say to her."

Sighing, Harper could see his point, but it pissed him off that he had to explain himself. "I left. It wasn't anything that she did. I left because the ghosts were dogging me and I was about to tip over the edge. I needed distance."

"Ah, I get it."

And Harper knew he probably did. Chad was his boss, but also a man he considered a true friend. He'd been through his own ordeals.

Tiredness was once again dragging at him. "Did we get them all? Malone and all his hired guns?"

"I believe we did, yes."

"Good," Harper sighed.

Chad squeezed his arm. "I'll be back to see you in a bit. I think Cat went down to the cafeteria. Food's not too bad here so I may join her."

Harper gave him a thumbs up, energy fading fast. "Tell her she's beautiful for me."

Chad laughed as he walked out the door. "I will."

CAT WAS PICKING at a chicken salad when Harper's boss stopped beside her at the table. "Mind if I join you?"

She waved a hand at the empty booth across from her. "Not at all."

Chad set his tray down first, then shimmied into the open bench. Cat lifted her eyebrows at the food piled on his tray. "Are you really going to eat all that?"

Grinning, he shook his head. "Probably not. Thought I might take one of the sandwiches up to Harper when I was done."

She smiled, appreciating that her husband had considerate friends. "I'm sure he'll eat it. The man will eat anything."

Chad nodded, biting into a chicken sandwich. He chewed thoughtfully for a couple of minutes, then met her eyes. "He said to tell you you looked beautiful today."

Cat looked down at the table, sudden tears blurring her vision. When they'd been living together like a real family he had told her all the time that he loved her. And every day, without fail, he told her how beautiful she was. She could be scrubbing toilets or landscaping, anything, and he would walk up to her, cup her face in his huge hands and tell her how beautiful she was.

As the wife of a Navy SEAL she'd gotten used to the long absences and doing things for herself. But when Harper came home he'd made the most of every day, telling her everything she'd missed hearing while he was gone.

Was this some kind of subtle message that he wanted to be with her again? Or was she looking for rainbows on a rainy day?

She sent Chad a sad smile. "That's one of those couple things that you miss when you're separated, you know. All the little ways he paid attention."

Chad frowned. "Yeah. I'm going to have to head back to Denver soon. My soon-to-be wife is waiting patiently for me. I felt like I had to be here for Harper though, because he didn't have any family. If you're going to stick around..."

He trailed off and she knew what he was asking.

"I'll be here for a while. Till he kicks me out. Or tries to," she grinned.

Chad laughed, nodding appreciatively. "I think you may be able to give our man a run for his money. I'll plan on leaving tomorrow, then. Not sure what Duncan will do."

Cat nodded, a little worried about being left alone with her own husband. When she was the only support he had would he resent her for that fact?

DUNCAN HADN'T RETURNED by the time they entered the room. Harper appeared to still be asleep. His jaw was as relaxed as she'd seen it since she'd been here. When he woke, everything would get hard again.

She huffed at the thought, her eyes scanning down his body. It would be a while before he'd be thinking about *that* again.

Chad sat in the chair at the back of the room and allowed her the one beside the bed.

Cat's eyes scanned the IV. He'd need fluid again soon. There was a tray on the bedside table. She lifted the lid. Nothing had been touched.

"They wanted to feed me like a baby," Harper growled.

She should have known he wouldn't allow that. And she should have known he wasn't asleep. Picking up the coffee mug of clear broth she placed it in his free hand. "If you can keep this down for a little while we'll give you something more substantial. Chad brought you a sandwich, but we have to make sure your stomach is solid. You just had surgery. You're probably going to be passing gas, too."

For the first time he grinned. Oh, she'd missed that reckless, irreverent, fleeting flash of teeth. "Check."

Cat couldn't help but grin as well. She squeezed his arm and sat in the chair, content to wait while he worked on the broth. The first sip made him scowl.

"What the hell is this?"

"Just clear broth."

"Of what?"

She shrugged, then remembered that he would not be able to see that. "Not sure. I think just chicken. It's more about getting the fluid in you than anything."

Harper drank reluctantly. Cat knew the food was minimal but he really needed to start with something easy.

Once he emptied the mug and dropped it to the tray

he turned his head toward her expectantly.

"Let's wait and see how that settles."

It seemed to settle fine so she allowed him to have the chicken breast off the sandwich. He ate it in three huge bites and sat back against the bed. "That's better. I could do with about three more though."

Chad laughed. "Dude, you better make sure you can keep that down."

There was a knock on the door and Duncan's too-chipper voice greeted him. "Preston. You're looking better this evening."

Duncan tapped him on the closest leg.

Harper nodded. "Hey, boss."

Chad moved out of the chair and allowed Duncan to sit down. Cat watched him lower himself into the chair and forced herself to keep the cringe of sympathy internal. Every movement he made looked like it hurt. The brackets around his mouth had been there a long time. And in spite of his jovial voice it didn't look like he'd been sleeping very much either.

"I called the office. Palmer said to tell you to do what you need to do then get back to work. The other guys said to tell you hi, too."

Harper nodded. "I'd be out of here now if I could."

"I think you may be here a while," Cat told him. "At least a couple more days. You just had surgery. Or until the surgeon checks your eyes and tells us otherwise."

He started to fold his arms over his heavy chest, then stopped in the middle and let them rest back on the mattress.

Cat watched the skin of his jaw pale. He'd forgotten about the gunshot wound.

Rubbing her forehead Cat forced back a yawn, suddenly struck by tiredness. She'd been here twenty-four seven for the past couple days.

"Why don't you go back to your hotel and chill for a while?"

Cat looked at him in surprise. Even unsighted he had the sharpest senses she'd ever seen. "I think I may. I'll be back in the morning."

Then came the awkward point when she didn't know how to say goodbye. Did she kiss him? Squeeze his hand? Fuck it. Leaning down, she pressed a kiss to a clear spot on his cheek. "If you need anything the nurses have my number."

He nodded and clutched her hand. For a moment it felt like he wasn't going to let her go, then, abruptly, he did. "I'll be fine."

And she knew he would be. It was just so natural for her to worry about him.

"I'll stick around for a few hours."

Cat gave Duncan an appreciative look. "Thank you. I thought you might."

Chad stepped forward to take her hand. "I have to go back to Denver for a while, but I'll be back in a few days if he's still here."

"You people are talking about me as if I'm not even here. I don't need babysitters."

Cat shared a wince with the other men.

"Quit it," Harper snapped.

Cat laughed and turned to leave the room. "I'll be back tomorrow, big guy."

Harper mumbled a goodbye.

She paused for just a moment, wanting to cross and give him a kiss like she used to. Then she forced the urge away and left. They weren't in a place to do that yet.

Cat didn't blame him for being pissed. If she were in his position she'd be aggravated too. Unable to see anything or anyone would be beyond frustrating.

Rather than take a cab to the hotel, she made herself walk the few blocks to the Marriot. Sitting in the hospital room for so long hadn't done her body any good. By the time she got back to the hotel room she was feeling whipped. She'd reached her limit. Plugging her cell phone into the charger and setting the alarm, she dropped to the bed face down, exhausted.

HARPER WANTED TO get up and pace. Sitting in the fucking bed was making him insane. Yes, there was pain, but he could block that out. It was early morning so the hospital was quiet too, which made it all the worse. One of the nurses had turned the TV on for him, but he'd gotten pissed when he couldn't figure out how to change the channel. Now he was listening to an infomercial on hair removal. And gritting his teeth in frustrated fury.

Chad and Duncan had left last night a couple hours after Cat and for the first time in a long time he'd felt completely alone. As a sniper you got used to your own company. If you had a spotter with you, great, but for the past year working at LNF he'd been without. Now that he was injured, with no vision, he felt at the mercy of the world. An afterthought.

He heard the hiss of the door as it slid open.

"You're awake already? I kind of figured you would be."

Harper could have wept at the sound of Cat's morning-husky voice. She was the only one who knew he loved to be up at the ass-crack of dawn. Many, many times over the years he'd been in the military she'd gotten up with him, made him breakfast and coffee and sent him on his way. Sometimes she'd been the one to wake him up because she was a natural early riser as well.

"I need you to get me the fuck out of here," he rasped.

She must have heard the desperation in his voice because he heard her drop her things to the chair beside the bed. "Let me talk to a nurse."

"I don't care what the nurse says," he grumbled. "I need to walk and I can't do that without bumbling around like an idiot."

"I know that," she said patiently, cranking his ire. "But you can't walk around with your ass hanging in the air. That johnny barely fits you."

Oh. That did make sense. Shit.

So he set his jaw and waited as she went out and sweet-talked somebody into bringing him a pair of scrubs pants. The nurse that brought them also took the irritating IV out of his arm. They'd taken his catheter out the night before, to his never-ending relief. "Now," she told him sternly, "no bending over, no running and until you're more steady, no stairs. We would prefer you stay on this floor, but as long as your wife is with you you can go down to the cafeteria. The doctor should be here later this morning to take a look at you, so don't get lost."

He almost saluted the crotchety old woman. Turning in the bed, he let his feet drop to the floor. He'd fumbled his way to the bathroom once already, dragging the IV pole, so he knew he could hold his weight. The disorientation was what got him.

The nurse seemed satisfied that he wasn't going to keel over so she fitted him with a sling for his left arm. "I know it's not comfortable but if you're out of bed you need to wear this, otherwise you're going to rip something open." He grimaced but she patted him on the cheek like a child and left him alone with Cat. He heard her whisper something to her on the way out the door.

"What did she say?" he demanded.

Cat snorted. "That you've got a nice ass."

"No, she didn't," he snapped.

She laughed. "No, she said you were stubborn."

That he could believe, but he didn't care. Stubborn had served him well all his life.

Harper patted around on the bed beside him, then held the scrubs out toward Cat. "She said I'm not allowed to bend over."

Silence met his statement and it was several long seconds before she took the pants from his hand. Harper shrugged the gown off and threw it toward the bed, then waited to see what her response would be now that he was standing in front of her naked. Fuck, he wished he could see.

"Looks like you've been bulking up," she murmured.

He grinned when he heard the huskiness in her voice and incredibly, even with all the nasty shit going on, the aches and pain and vulnerability, his body began to respond. "Yeah, I have."

He felt her body heat as she moved in front of him and knelt down. Blood surged and he knew she was getting an eyeful, but the proximity was totally his undoing. Even without his sight Cat was the sexiest woman he'd ever been near. Just the sound of her voice, so dear after not hearing it for so long, made him ache.

Her fingers pressed on his right ankle and he lifted his foot, then his left. As she began to draw the pants up his legs, then his hips, he wondered how far she would go. All the way apparently. The elastic scraped over his erection as she settled the waistband at his hips and tightened the drawstring. Before she pulled away though, she shocked the hell out of him by cupping him in her hand. "It's very nice to touch you again, Harper."

He wanted to pull her into his arms and find her mouth, but her warmth moved away. And that was probably the smartest thing she could do. Guilt turned his stomach as he thought about his situation. What business did he have encouraging anything between them? Nothing had really changed.

She took his right hand and placed it on her shoulder. "I'm going to lead you out of the room, okay? You are on my left shoulder. I'll make sure I walk wide around things. There's a nice patio just outside the cafeteria. We'll head there. Sound good?"

"Yes."

Anything sounded good compared to staying in this freaking room.

She was as careful as she promised to be and he could tell there were people walking wide of them. It made his skin creep that he couldn't see what they were doing, but he trusted Cat to watch his six. She paused at the end of the hallway. "Are you doing okay? Want to stop for a minute?"

He did but he wouldn't admit that to her. "I'm fine. Keep going."

When they got on the elevator he didn't expect the vertigo that hit when it started down. He swayed and clutched at the slick walls but almost immediately Cat was there, wedging herself beneath his good shoulder and bracing her feet. Harper tried not to rest on her too much but the weakness in his knees about took him down. When they landed at the bottom she stayed propped against him, not moving. "We'll go when you're ready."

Harper dragged in oxygen and waited for his head to stop spinning. "I'm ready."

The elevator doors had already closed so she pressed the button to open them and came back. When she tried to position his hand he reached a few inches farther and settled his hand at the nape of her neck, on the right side. It placed them in a closer proximity, but her hips brushing against his as they walked was really very nice.

The awareness from earlier surged back. It had been more than a year since they'd been together. Seventeen months and three weeks, actually.

And I can only blame myself.

As soon as she led him through a set of automatic doors he could smell and feel the cool, fresh air. He dragged it in, filling his lungs, until a sharp pain ripped through his chest from the movement. She led him to a table and put his hand on one armrest of a wrought iron chair. Ever so carefully he lowered himself down in. Cat moved to his right. "You're on a paved patio with four sets of tables and chairs. A concrete path winds through some little trees to the left and it looks like it leads to a longer walking path. There are seven people out here right now, mostly nurses. And, of course, your back is to the wall."

If he hadn't had the bandages on his eyes he would have gotten a little choked up again. She knew exactly what he would have looked at when he entered the area. "Thank you," he murmured.

They sat for a while just enjoying the sun and fresh air but Harper knew they had things to talk about. He just hated to drag them up. He took as deep of a breath as his chest would allow.

"How's Dillon?"

Silence stretched between them and he wondered if she'd even respond.

"She's fine. Growing like a weed. Becoming a young woman."

Harper swallowed hard, devastation rolling through

him. He thought he wanted to know but maybe he didn't. Fuck. The thought of the time that he had lost with his almost teenage daughter was the greatest regret of his life.

"I told her you were on a long assignment. She told me the other day though, that she thinks you're dead and I'm just scared to tell her. She hasn't heard from you for a long time. Neither one of us has."

Whether she meant them to or not her words destroyed him, more even than the physical pain he was fighting.

"Tate," she continued, her voice matter of fact, "has stopped asking where you are because I give him the same answer over and over and over again."

"And what is that?" he growled.

"That Daddy will come home as soon as he is able to."

Though he had no sight he turned his head away from her to try to recover his breath. His teeth were clenched so hard something popped in his jaw. Being away from his kids devastated him, but they were safer with him not in the house.

After that last time getting shot up in Afghanistan he'd handed in his walking papers. Though he was only in his mid-thirties at that time he was a little old by SEAL standards. His kill record had been impeccable but the deployments were getting harder. Not just physically but mentally as well. Being shot that last time had been a hard recovery and he'd been tired. Not just body tired but spirit tired as well.

So once he'd recovered from being plugged he'd taken a training job on base. It hadn't been as exciting as hopping on a 'copter and taking off for parts unknown, but he'd still been immersed in the Teams lifestyle.

He'd had issues with paranoia though. When the guys left on deployment he worried the base would be attacked because it was less protected. When they were in-house he worried the base would be attacked. The terrorists had taken out bounties on all snipers' heads and he worried that he, himself, would draw danger to the States. To his family. When he'd been in the Teams the target on his back had felt so real. Distance hadn't helped. So he'd carried a weapon everywhere—grocery store, auto mechanics, kids' school until they'd posted no weapons, even for the servicemen. That paranoia, and an incident with Tate in the fall had led to his breaking point.

Cat had fought him when he'd threatened to leave. It had been the most bitter fight they'd ever had because they'd repeated it so many times. But the nightmare of waking up and seeing his four-year old son holding his loaded side arm out to his sleeping wife, barrel first, had literally terrified him. He'd kept the M11 Sig Sauer 9mm on the bedside table beside him at night because he had dreams of being caught unaware by terrorists. Cat hadn't liked it, but she'd understood his need to feel safe when he was home. In the desert or wherever he was sent, he had the weapon on or mere inches away twenty-four seven. It was difficult to try to give it up when he came home after so many years of his life depending upon keeping it close.

That night had cemented in his head how wrong it was for him to subject his kids to his neuroses. If the kids needed Cat in the night they'd go straight to the master bedroom where they slept. First he'd gotten an apartment a few blocks away, coming home for dinner and seeing the kids off to school in the mornings then going to training, but that had seemed to confuse them. For a couple of weeks they carried on that jagged schedule until Cat had put her foot down. He needed to move back into the house. They would deal with his issues together as a family, get counseling. But he hadn't done it. Their safety was paramount and he just couldn't be near them.

"Hawthorn and the others still come over to check on us sometimes. His little boy is on the T-ball team with Tate. And Katey and Lucas have us over for dinner occasionally."

Gratitude tightened Harper's throat, making it hard to swallow. He couldn't be there in Virginia but his Team had stepped in like they'd promised they would. They'd carried his Swiss-cheesed, two hundred and seventy pound ass out of Kandahar and they were still carrying him three years later. Every once in a while his phone would ping with a message from one of the guys but he very rarely responded. Then the longer the stretch of time went the harder it was to respond.

Like the stretch of time now. He knew Cat was waiting on some kind of acknowledgement of what she'd told him but his brain was shorting out. He wasn't ready to deal with their issues.

"Katey's still putting up with Lucas's foul mouth, huh?"

She didn't respond for several long seconds and he knew he'd disappointed her again.

"Yes, she is. They got married several months ago. And Katey is pregnant."

He forced his lips to smile, though his gut churned. "They'll be great parents."

"Hm, maybe," she murmured. "I thought we were going to be great parents, too."

If she'd leveled a shotgun on him and fired, she couldn't have hurt him more than she did right then.

Cat had a right to be pissed. When he'd married her years ago she'd known being with the Teams took most of his focus. Missions had taken him away for months at a time. He'd been deployed to Iraq four times and Afghanistan twice, each time for six months or more. Then there were too many individual ops to even count. Though the deployments were hard Cat took care of everything like she'd been doing it all along. And she had, actually. She was literally a single parent. He hadn't been at Dillon's birth or Tate's. Christmases had passed with barely a glance. If she hadn't have sent him a box of treats every holiday he wouldn't even have noticed them.

But even when he'd been physically home, mentally he hadn't. In his mind he'd always been preparing for the next op. He was on the range with his rifle every day, rain or shine. Training in the gym every day. Keeping that fine combat ready edge took a lot of grueling work.

The only thing he'd been able to do well for his family was leave. And provide for them monetarily.

"You are a great parent," he told her firmly.

She snorted in that derisive way she had. "Doesn't feel like it sometimes."

Harper couldn't help her with this because he felt like a failure all the time.

"Anyway," she sighed. "We're going to sit out here for a while and enjoy the day. Then we're going to go back up to the room to talk to the doctor and he's going to change our lives with his incredible news. Sound okay to you?"

He nodded slightly, willing to go along with her fairy tale for a little while.

CHAPTER THREE

WHEN THEY ARRIVED back at his room Harper was more whipped than he wanted to let on, but he forced one foot in front of the other. The grumpy nurse came in and told them that the doctor had just been in looking for them. She hurried out of the room to try to find him.

Harper hiked himself onto the bed but didn't recline. Even though it caused some pain through his chest, he sat up straight at the edge of the mattress. The clock on the wall ticked and he counted off the seconds as they waited. Cat paced the room, moving from one side of the cramped space to the other. He almost snapped at her to stop but he realized she needed the release as well. If he didn't think he'd bang into things he would be pacing as well.

The door hissed open and his heart raced before he could settle it back.

"Mrs. Preston, Harper. I'm Dr. Coughlin. How are you feeling today?"

Harper almost cursed at the ridiculous question. How did he think he felt? "Like I'm going to peel my skin off if I don't get some answers."

The doctor laughed a little and Harper felt him move

in front of him. "Well then, let's see what's going on behind these bandages."

Harper held himself as still as he could as the doctor started to fiddle with the bandages over his eyes. He curled his fists into the mattress, attacked by a wave of trepidation. Before the feeling could completely register Cat had curled one of her hands over his own.

If he could have given her a look he would have. Instead he flipped his hand over and crushed hers within it.

The doctor took his sweet time removing all the wraps around his head. Harper couldn't tell if he was doing it deliberately or not. The man murmured to the returning nurse and he felt the weight of the heaviest bandages leave his head.

"Now Harper, I'm going to remove the last layers slowly. Be patient, because we're going to dim the room. We don't want your eyes to hurt you more than they already will."

He nodded slightly, jaw clamped, and fought off the choking impatience.

As the air of the room hit his skin for the first time in days Harper took a huge breath, in spite of the pain to his chest, and opened his eyes.

Pain immediately brought the tears. Tissues were pressed into his hands and he blotted at his streaming eyes, but they wouldn't stop leaking.

"This is very normal after a trauma like you've had. Just give them a minute to acclimatize."

Harper mopped his face but the tears kept coming. After a couple of long minutes they began to ease and he blinked his eyes open again. Everything was super blurry, but even through the blurriness he knew one thing.

The fairy tale was over.

He turned his head to the left, hoping that the first thing he would see would be Cat. And it was. She'd cut her hair since the last time he'd seen her and the dark strands curled around the back of her ears. Her face was red as if she were fighting tears silently.

But that information was drawn in from his left eye. His right, dominant eye was completely black.

The doctor must have sensed his discouragement because he launched into several tests that made him focus on the man. Harper did what he could but when the doctor requested he cover his left eye with his hand and to tell him what he was holding up, Harper couldn't keep his mouth shut any longer.

"I don't see a fucking thing. No color, no variations of gray, no blurriness, nothing. It's a black screen."

Cat's hand tightened on his own as his voice got whisper quiet. She knew he was beyond pissed.

The doctor threw out platitudes about giving his eye time to recover and they could look at transplants but Harper shut down. He heard Cat's calm voice asking about second opinions then the doctor's affronted reply, and he almost smiled. His wife would do everything in her power to make things right, no matter who she offended. It was one of the many million things he loved about her, that mama-bear attitude. "I need you to step outside for a minute, please," she told the doctor quietly.

Harper didn't hear them leave. Thoughts of going

through life lopsided, perpetually off balance crowded into his mind. Diego, a Marine at LNF, had lost his eye in an IED attack years ago and he still had balance issues.

How the fuck was he supposed to do his job?

Cat stepped in close, wedging herself between his knees. She cupped his face in her strong hands and forced him to look at her. "You need to breathe. This is not the end of the world. In spite of what you think, your fucking right eye is not your life."

Harper dragged in a huge gulp of air, only then realizing he'd stilled as if readying for a shot, though his heart raced in panic. Nodding at her words, he forced his heartbeat to slow down. "What the hell am I going to do?"

In spite of the world falling around them, she smiled that beautiful, soul-shattering smile she had. "You're going to move to a different position in your company with different tasks. Or you're going to learn to shoot with your other eye. It's that easy."

Was it really though?

Cat tightened her hands on his face and leaned forward to press kisses to his cheeks. She paused at the corner of his right eye and pressed a lingering kiss there, then moved to wrap her arms around his neck in a fierce hug. "You're still gorgeous and you're still a bad-ass mother fucker," she whispered into his ear. "That eye is such a small part of you."

Harper wrapped his arms around her, so grateful that she'd managed to find him and be here. The news he had just received would have devastated him and he wondered what would have happened if she hadn't been here to calm him as she always had. He would have punched someone or broken something. Hell, maybe both. His iron control only held so far. Cat was the only thing that kept him sane.

And when he thought about it rationally he knew she was right. Since he'd been out of the service his sniping skills had fallen to the wayside for the most part. Duncan used him more for personal protection and investigation than anything else. He used his size to be intimidating when he needed to, and his mind when it was more appropriate. It was just hard because he identified himself as a SEAL, as being a sniper. He had for years.

No, losing his vision wasn't the end of the world. It just felt like it right now.

Cat pulled away and looked up at him. Even in the dim light he could see the determination flashing in her whiskey golden eyes. "We'll get a second opinion."

Harper nodded but he was distracted. Lifting his hand, he fingered her dark hair. It was so short in the back and cut at an edgy angle. "When did you cut it?"

She looked a little unsure but lifted her chin. "Several months ago."

He blinked and turned his head a little to look her up and down. Still tall and willowy, just tall enough to reach his own chin, but she looked a little leaner. As if the time apart from him had been hard on her. Her big, eloquent eyes still dominated her angular face, and if they were any less beautiful she would have looked harsh.

The makeup she had worn today had smudged beneath her eyes, as if she'd been crying. He hadn't heard her make a sound. Reaching up, he wiped the evidence away with his thumbs, then as naturally as breathing, he leaned down to press a kiss to her lips.

"You look stunning today."

Cat froze and her breath stilled. Harper cupped her jaw and leaned into her, desperate to find that connection they'd had before. And it was there. When she leaned into him and moved her mouth they fell into the rhythm naturally. He realized that he felt nervous. If she pushed him away he wouldn't blame her. Honestly, he didn't know how she'd put up with him all these years, in and out of her life all the time. In his heart he knew he had always taken more than he gave and it made him feel ashamed.

Like he was doing now.

On that sobering thought he pulled back.

"You're thinking too hard," she admonished. "I can see it in your face. And you need to stop. It was just a kiss."

But her kisses turned him on like nothing else in the world. Once she got a glimpse of the scrubs she would know too. It had been a long time since he'd held her, kissed her, loved her. His body knew that release was inches away. They just had a lot of issues.

Cat narrowed her eyes at him. "You're still thinking too hard."

He barked out a laugh. "Probably," he admitted. "But it's the way I am."

She nodded and smiled. "But you don't have to be."

Harper wished he could rid himself of the anxiety that plagued him. Working out helped take the edge off, but he hadn't been able to do that for a solid week now. Damn, had he really been in the hospital that long? He glanced around the room. There was a whiteboard across the way that gave the date and his nurses' names. Yep. A week. His gaze fell to the rolling table beside his bed and the tattered brown teddy bear resting there.

"Your boss said the little girl you saved wanted you to have it while you were sick, but she expects to get it back."

Emotion constricted his throat and he had to look away from Cat to clear it. Reaching out a finger, he stroked down the stuffed animal's head. "She didn't have to do that."

"Chad seemed very surprised she had given it up."

He nodded, his head throbbing from emotion and physical pain. He wanted to crawl into bed and drag Cat with him.

She seemed to sense as well that he had almost reached his limit, because she peeled the blankets back on the bed. "Why don't you chill for a little bit? We'll go over our options later. Want me to help you with the sling?"

Without argument he turned to let her release the Velcro strips, then shifted himself back to the mattress, dragging a spare pillow over his aching eyes. The lack of light immediately eased some of the tension in his head. "Can you hang out with me for a while?"

She stroked her hand down his arm and squeezed his fingers. "I will."

Huffing out a breath, he tried to let everything go.

CAT KNEW THE second Harper drifted off to sleep. His fingers slackened their death grip on her hand just slightly and the pillow he'd rested over his eyes slipped to the mattress. She pulled away without his noticing.

God, he looked bad. Now that she knew he was asleep she allowed the tight rein on her emotions to slacken as she took him in. His handsome face looked like he had gone ten rounds with a heavyweight champ. There was bruising around both of his deep-set eyes and down his long nose. Several cuts and suture lines circled his right eye. The scarring would be significant.

The tight skull cut he usually clipped his hair in had grown out and was a little shaggy. The dark black hair was the longest she'd seen it in years. Long meaning business-short, just not bad-ass sniper short like he usually preferred it.

Gaze dancing down his chest, she sighed and wiped her leaking eyes. At least he was in one piece. Everything else could be dealt with.

The doctor probably wanted to know what their thoughts were. Crossing the dim room, taking a last deep breath she eased the door open as quietly as she could.

The eye surgeon sat at the nurse's station, tapping notes into a computer. He looked up when she rested her arms on the counter above him. "What are the chances he will ever get the sight back in that eye? Is a transplant an option? No bullshit."

The doctor looked a little affronted that she spoke to him that way but she had no more patience. The man stood up and circled the counter to wave her to a small seating area. Cat stalked to the chairs and sat, then waited for him to answer her questions.

"I think there is a very slim chance of recovering vision in that eye. Yes, you can pursue second opinions and we will absolutely do everything in our power to make it happen, but in my twelve years of practicing I have not seen an eye as damaged as your husband's recover. We can put him on a corneal transplant list but the tissue around the cornea is damaged as bad as the cornea itself. If he struggles with infection in that eye, there is a very real possibility that the eye itself will have to be removed."

Cat sat back in the chair. She'd definitely gotten her answers. But he hadn't told her anything she hadn't expected. The fears had been in her heart; she just didn't want Harper to know that.

"So, what do we do now?"

The doctor leaned back in the chair and crossed his legs. "Right now your husband isn't even at a place in his recovery that I can recommend him for the transplant list. We need to get a little ways out and deal with the infections that I'm sure will come. He had serious trauma to that eye. There's a chance he could still have glass in it we just couldn't see. It's not going to be a quick fix. He'll be on heavy antibiotics and pain medication for a while."

She nodded her head and sighed. "How long does he need to stay?"

"Well, I'll consult with his primary care team. Whenever they think he can be released he can be, and we'll follow up later. Or I can transfer his care over to another doctor where you live."

Cat blinked and rubbed her hand over her forehead. There was so much to think about.

"When he is released," the doctor continued, "I suggest you drive wherever you go. The pressure change in an airplane could damage him further."

She nodded her head and shook his hand, then he left. The fact that she had just had all her fears confirmed made her sad. She knew the responsibility of talking to Harper would fall to her. And she would have to hurt him again.

On the bright side, there was a road trip in their future.

Exploring had always been one of their passions. It had started out as a SEAL's need to reconnoiter the area, but she had joined him and added some fun to the task. They used to drive for hours wandering from state to state, sometimes only getting back minutes before he was due to report for duty. That had been when they were young and a little more carefree. Not that she'd ever tell her daughter, but Dillon had been conceived in the back of Harper's old truck on one of his quick trips home.

Two or three years ago they'd gone on a camping road trip. Two weeks in the middle of nowhere. Tate had been small then, maybe only three, and Dillon had been old enough that she'd resented leaving her friends. But they had all ended up enjoying themselves. It was one of the last clear memories she had of them doing something fun as a family. Dillon's too. Tate didn't remember it at all, which made her sad.

How long she sat in that chair reminiscing, she didn't know. But when a nurse took off running in the direction of Harper's room she knew something was up. She bolted for the door. As she pushed through she heard him yell at them to get the fuck away from him. Harper stood on the far side of the room, bloodshot eyes wild, arm dripping blood where he'd caught it on something. Cat grabbed the back of one of the nurse's scrubs as she tried to reach for him and jerked the woman back. "You need to get out of here. Now. I'll talk to him."

The nurses argued with her, but Cat could outlast them all. "Get out!" They finally seemed to respond to the authority in her voice. They scuttled out of the room, tugging a sobbing young girl with them.

Cat took a deep breath and waited for Harper's anger to ease. He had fallen into a fighting stance, arms outstretched, ready to defend himself. She didn't need to wonder what had set him off so thoroughly. It looked like one of the nurse assistants had come in to do something, flicked the light on and scared the crap out of Harper.

His bloodshot eyes were blinking and he scowled fiercely, obviously in pain. Cat flicked the light switch down, plunging the room into as much darkness as she could. There was a nightlight in the bathroom casting a dim glow and a sliver of daylight beyond the blinds, but other than that the room was dark.

"Harper, you need to get a hold of yourself. It's just me in here now and I've dimmed the lights. What happened?"

His stance relaxed and his big head tilted toward her. Tears streaked his cheeks and she knew the pain had to be excruciating. Plucking several tissues from the box on the table, she approached him. "I have tissues I'm going to give you, okay? And your arm is bleeding. We need to make it stop. Okay, babe?"

"Yeah," he croaked, obviously hurting. He held a hand out for the tissues. "I'm sorry I went off. She flicked on the lights and before I knew what was going on she had started doing things with my chest bandage. I didn't hear her come in."

Cat felt sick to her stomach. "I was sitting just outside, but I didn't see her go in either. I'm sorry about that. I was supposed to be on duty and I dropped the ball."

He leaned against the bed, hands over his face. "You weren't on duty. I'm not a child."

She knew he wasn't but the guilt still nagged at her. Lost in memories, she hadn't seen the woman enter the room.

"I'm going to touch you on the shoulder, okay?"

When her hand landed on the tense deltoid muscle, he reached up, grabbed her hand and dragged her into his heavy arms. Cat knew the hug was for his own peace of mind, but she savored the touch. For just a few seconds she allowed herself to burrow into his chest, the scalding heat of his skin wrapping her in a heavy cocoon.

It was no surprise to hear the strident knock on the door of the room a few minutes later.

"I'd better go smooth some feathers."

Even in the dim light she could see the flash of his white teeth as he grinned. "Just like old times, huh?"

Cat snorted. "Absolutely."

When she returned to the room, Harper literally growled when she told him he would have to have another exam. But when the doctor came in he'd calmed to icy fury. Cat winced at the angry red torn skin around the bullet hole in his chest. The entrance wound had been trimmed and stitched, but they'd had to do surgery to remove the bullet. It had wedged against his shoulder blade in the back. The doctor had been amazed that the blade itself hadn't been shattered.

Now, though, a couple of those external stitches had ripped out. Harper didn't say anything as the area was numbed and re-stitched. In total there were now twenty-eight stitches in his chest.

Actually, the incident paved the way for his early release. Cat knew she had to get Harper out of there, not only for his peace of mind but her own as well. The primary care physician was a little hesitant, but when she assured him that he would have the same care just away from the hospital he seemed to relax a bit. When she hinted at the liability issues they were both dancing around, he agreed that Harper could be released, but only after a final night of rest.

Though he frowned at the delay, Harper seemed to understand that it was in his best interest. The hospital quieted down and for the most part the nurses left them alone that evening.

Duncan came later that night and sat with him. They told him about their plans to leave and he nodded in understanding. "Yeah, I wouldn't stay here any longer than I had to either," he admitted.

Harper felt bad for making Duncan sit here so long. The hospital brought up memories for all of them and h couldn't wait to get out.

Cat went back to the hotel and crashed. Once again, though, she returned at the ass-crack of dawn.

The doctor also showed up early.

"I want you to wear your sling as much as possible and to avoid showers for a couple more days," the doctor told them. "I'm sending you out with a couple of anti-inflammatory, pain and antibiotic prescriptions, but if you have issues with the wound, go to a hospital."

Cat took all the aftercare paperwork and folded it away into her purse. One of the nurses knocked on the door and entered, carrying a bulky looking package. With a dirty look at Cat, she handed it to the doctor and quickly left.

Ripping the package open the doctor handed a set of dark glasses to Harper. "I know these are not fashionable, but you need to wear them. It will help with the sunlight and allow your healthy eye a chance to relax. It's going to be doing double duty. Rest as much as you can and expect headaches."

The longer he talked the more impatient Harper became. The average person probably wouldn't notice the tightening of his jaw or the weight of his animosity in the air, but Cat did.

"Thank you so much, doctor. We really do appreciate the care we've received here."

The man seemed to take the dismissal as exactly that and disappeared through the door shortly thereafter.

Less than a half hour later they were in the main lobby. Cat was amazed at how quickly they'd let him loose. Days ago she'd gone to a local mall and bought Harper a couple of outfits at the big men's store, knowing that he would need something when he walked out. She was very glad she had now, otherwise he'd have been leaving in scrubs.

When she handed him the final item though, his jaw worked and he wouldn't look at her for a long time. "I didn't have time to grab one of yours when I left but I found this in one of those outdoor stores the other day."

Harper opened the blade of the Kershaw knife. It wasn't nearly as big as what he was used to carrying, but it was as big as she wanted to get him. He tested the weight of the blade and the sharpness of the edge before clipping it into the corner of his pocket. When he looked up there was appreciation in his expression. "You have no idea how much I've missed having something there. Thank you."

Cat actually did have some idea. His hand had gone to his hip several times over the past few days, whether he realized it or not. "You're welcome. Just don't flash it at the nurses."

He chuckled then winced, holding his chest with his un-slung arm. "What are they going to do, kick me out?"

Cat laughed. "I think they're already kicking us out early. They just don't want to deal with your temper tantrums. God forbid you hit one of their scrawny asses. You'd break them."

He grimaced and she felt bad for being a wet blanket. Turning away, she left the room.

CHAPTER FOUR

WHILE SHE WENT for the car, he sat in the obligatory exit wheelchair glowering at the world. At least she assumed he was glowering. He'd put the bulky glasses on almost immediately when they hit the sunlight. The orderly with him kept trying to talk, but Harper was not in the mood. She could almost feel the hostility rolling off him.

When she finally returned with the big GMC Yukon, the only vehicle she thought he would be comfortable riding in, he shoved himself out of the chair and stalked across the few feet of pavement. Cat wondered if he'd hurt his chest doing that—not that he'd let her know if he had. The sling was on his arm, but she didn't expect it to stay there very long.

Cat put the SUV into drive and pulled out of the lot. She wanted to ask Harper if he was feeling okay, but his head was tipped back against the rest and he was breathing deeply, as if he couldn't get enough of the fresh air.

"I couldn't breathe in that place," he admitted.

Cat marveled at his senses. Even with his eyes closed he'd known she was looking at him. That crazy sixth-sense of his kicking in. "Completely understandable. You have a lot of not so great memories in there. In several hospitals in several states and several countries."

Harper grinned, the flash of teeth bold and vibrant. "At least this hospital wasn't being bombed like the one I went through in Iraq."

"Or in the path of a once in a lifetime blizzard like the time you were at Walter Reed."

He gave her a nod, his smile fading. "You've been at most of them with me. I appreciate that, Cat."

Wow. She sucked in a breath at his softly spoken words. "I was your wife. Where else would I have been?"

Harper rocked his head toward her. "You could have stayed home like a lot of the wives did."

She shook her head, grimacing. "That's not where a wife belongs when her husband is hurt. She belongs at his side. Rooting him on to recover as fully as possible."

"There were a lot of guys that had no one, either in Germany or when they got home."

"I know," she admitted. "But with my parents living within easy driving distance, I had an advantage. They were always ready to watch the kids at a second's notice."

He was quiet for a long time then, but his head was still turned toward her. With those dark glasses on she couldn't tell if he was awake or not.

Navigating the Amarillo streets she'd gotten used to over the past few days, she headed toward the interstate on-ramp. They would head north toward Denver for a little while, then they had a break in the middle at Cañon City. She hadn't told him about renting the house and thought it best not to now. They needed to take some time together, out of the hospital environment.

It would be neutral ground where they could talk about things.

As she accelerated up the onramp of 287 North, he rolled his head on the seat again and leaned forward, hand on his brow.

"Are you okay?" she asked. "Do I need to pull over?"

"No. Just some nausea. Keep going."

Cat kept driving but she kept one eye on him the entire time. Eventually he settled back against the seat. "Do you mind if I lay this seat back? I think if I lay down I may feel better."

"Absolutely. There's a blanket on the seat behind mine. If you can reach that you can use it for your head."

It was an easy reach for his long arm normally, but with the sling on he had to be careful. When he did drag the blanket to him, he used it to cover his head completely. Cat frowned at the weird shape, but whatever he needed to do...

They drove for a few hours and had crossed into the upper corner of New Mexico when she stopped for gas and a bite to eat. Harper roused and dragged the blanket from his head, blinking sleepily. The glasses had come off under the blanket and he fumbled to get them back on to fight the afternoon sun.

"I'm sorry I conked out on you."

Cat smiled at him as she pulled into the parking spot at a little but surprisingly busy restaurant connected to the gas station. "You're fine. You should rest as much as you possibly can."

They slid out of the vehicle and Cat watched to make sure he was steady on his feet. When he wavered just a bit she stepped close and wrapped her arm around his waist on the right, uninjured side. Harper shifted as if to nudge her away, but Cat held on. "Just go with it, stubborn."

There was a grumble of laughter before his heavy arm landed on her shoulders. "Fine, stubborn. But if I go down we're both going down."

After those first couple of wavering steps he actually steadied out pretty well. Cat didn't think he needed her support at all, but she kept her arm around him anyway, as if they were a couple out for a stroll. She was enjoying the contact with his hard body too much.

They entered the front door of the café and the hostess/waitress walked them back to a table Cat motioned to. It was the dimmest in the restaurant, so it would have to do. After the waitress left to get their drink orders, Harper slipped the glasses off the bridge of his nose and rubbed the area with his fingers. There were red marks on the high part of his nose where the glasses had rubbed. When the waitress returned he slipped them back on.

The woman handed them a couple of sticky menus and left to take care of other customers before returning to take their orders. The poor woman was run ragged, but gave them a smile as she scribbled on the pad. She promised to have the food out as soon as possible.

"How far have we driven?"

"Just a few hours, but I needed to get out and stretch. And get gas. This Yukon is a gas-guzzler. There's not a lot through here on this stretch of interstate."

Nodding a little, he stirred the ice cubes in his water glass. "It is pretty desolate," he agreed. "We should get into Denver in a few hours. When you reach the outer belt I'll give you directions to my place."

Cat didn't say anything, just let him assume that was where they were going. She had other plans.

Their food came surprisingly quickly considering how busy the place was, and it was good hearty food. The cook in this little hardscrabble place had some talent.

Harper ate as if he hadn't seen food for a week. Which he kind of hadn't. It was hard to get excited about hospital fare. The burger he had ordered was gone in a few big bites, as well as the fries.

Cat was not surprised when he ordered an extra serving of mashed potatoes and gravy and a slice of apple pie, then ploughed through that food when it came. Even working with only one hand he obliterated the mountain. When he finally sat back against the booth seat, she had to laugh at the somnolent look in his eyes. "Are you ready to go?" she asked.

Harper nodded. They paid the tab and left. Cat walked to the little attached gas station part and bought some snacks and a drink for the road, then they piled back into the Yukon. "I'm wide awake," she assured him. "Go ahead and sleep if you can. We may stop for the night somewhere along the way."

"Okay. Thanks, Cat." He ran his big hand down her shoulder. "This reminded me of our little road trips."

She nodded, throat tight. "Me too. I miss them."

He cleared his throat. "I do too."

With that he reclined his chair and bundled his head in the blanket again. Cat didn't know how he could breathe like that. Maybe breathing wasn't as important as keeping it dark to protect his eyes.

They drove for another three hours, long straight stretches of nothing. Once the sun went down Harper sat up and looked around. He winced and rubbed at his eyes. "I thought once the sun set I would be able to look around but I can't see much."

A car approached from the opposite direction, still the better part of a mile away. Cat watched Harper's reaction to the lights as they drew closer. When it got within a quarter mile he had to close his eyes and turn his head away.

"I wouldn't expect too much of yourself right now. You just got out of the hospital and are recovering from serious wounds. Don't stress about anything."

Harper didn't even glance at her, but he gave her a single nod. "I know that. It's just hard being so debilitated."

Cat could understand that. Harper Preston was the classic SEAL type—at the gym every day, eating fairly healthy, being the strongest man he could be, literally and figuratively. All of the other injuries he'd dealt with had been recoverable, no serious lasting effects. The loss of the vision in his eye would take him a while to deal with.

He stayed awake with her for the last part of the trip and when they pulled into Cañon City, he looked around in curiosity. Cat brought up the address of the house she'd rented on the GPS on her phone and followed the directions. The last of the twilight was dwindling away as they pulled up the drive twenty minutes later. It was just at the edge of the Temple Canyon Park and nestled on the slope of a mountain. The outdoor light was on but she couldn't see much of the house itself.

"What are we doing here? I thought we were going to stop at a hotel or something."

Cat shrugged and glanced at him, her heart pounding. "Not exactly. I rented this house for us for a while."

Harper scowled as he slid out of the SUV and circled the hood to meet her. "What do you mean you rented it 'for a while'? How long is a while?"

Cat slammed her door shut and moved to the passenger door where she'd stored her suitcase and his shopping bags. "Just what I said. A while. However long you give me. You can't go back to work yet anyway. I talked to Duncan and he says you need to take a couple weeks off at least. So I rented it for a couple weeks."

Dragging her suitcase across the paved drive she went to the lockbox visible at the side of the door and punched in a code. It popped open immediately and a gold key dropped into her hand. Cat let them inside the house but tried to follow only the illumination of nightlights positioned low along the hallways. When they reached the kitchen she moved to the glass-top stove, hoping there would be a light in the hood. It probably wouldn't be too sharp for Harper's eyes.

She tapped the button and the kitchen brightened.

The space was beautiful that she could see. Dark granite counter tops, pretty cherry cupboards, a side-by-side refrigerator. She opened the door. *Awesome!* The realtor had taken care of the essentials like she'd asked. Anything other than that she could drive into town for later.

Cat could feel Harper glaring at her from the kitchen doorway.

"Why didn't you tell me we weren't going back to Denver?"

Cat chuckled. "Well, you didn't really need to know. There's nothing you need to do here. No job, no responsibilities. I want you to recover. But I also want you to think about us, and the place we play in your life. You don't need to decide anything tonight, though. I'm going to find a bedroom and crash because I'm about to drop. Do your security check, because I know you won't rest being in a new environment without it. But do it quickly."

Crossing the kitchen, she leaned up to press a kiss to his stubborn, clamped jaw and disappeared down the hallway.

IT TOOK EVERYTHING he had in him to stand for her kiss and not grab her arms and shake her senseless. What the fuck was she thinking, bringing them out here in the middle of nowhere? He'd seen houses on the drive from Canón City, but not very many. The only thing that stopped him from yelling at her was the tiredness even he could see with his damn single eye in the slump of her shoulders and the droop of her mouth. She'd driven for seven hours today. He had slept most of that time and hadn't helped at all.

Harper looked around the space, then crossed to the patio doors he could see on the back wall. Finding the faceplate with his hand, he squinted his eyes in preparation of pain and flicked a switch. The light behind him came on, illuminating a heavy cherry wood dining set. He flicked the switch off then the one next to it up. Light illuminated a cement patio with a large swimming pool, then a rocky back yard beyond. Checking that the door was locked, he left the light on and moved to the next room.

Living room with more heavy wooden furniture, pale walls, a nice flat screen mounted on the wall beside a huge stone fireplace. Another set of patio doors leading to the pool area. He made sure they were locked then moved on. A bathroom was next, which he used before continuing. One bedroom, two, then a third. When he opened the door of the third Cat looked up in surprise, having just ripped her t-shirt over her head.

Harper stared at the swell of her breasts in the pink satin bra, his mouth suddenly watering. Fuck, it had been a long time. He didn't have a lot to be thankful for but in that moment he was extremely thankful he had the vision of at least one eye to see the beauty before him.

Cat lifted a dark brow in question. "My room is secure, Harper."

His cheeks heated. "Yeah, sorry."

Backing out of the room he pulled the door shut behind him, but he could still see her standing there, curves
lit by a soft bedside lamp. It was several long seconds
before he forced himself to release the doorknob.

The rest of the house seemed secure so he went to
one of the first bedrooms and stripped down. And
though he had the hard-on from hell and had slept most
of the way to Colorado, as soon as his head hit the pillow
he drifted away.

CAT WOKE SURPRISINGLY early. She figured she'd have
slept in, but excitement to meet the day urged her out of
bed. Hurrying through a nice, hot shower she combed
her short hair and dressed in jeans and a sweatshirt.
Padding to the kitchen in her bare feet, she found the
coffee maker. Damn. The sucker already had water in the
reservoir and coffee in the filter. She bumped the brew
switch and started going through the house.

The realtor had outdone herself. The house was
beautiful. And completely stocked. There were towels in
the cupboards, trash bags, cleaning supplies, everything
she needed for a stay. There were even spare toiletries in
the bathroom if they needed them. The refrigerator had
several types of meat and various accompaniments. It
had been expensive to rent the house this way, but she
prayed that it would do the job she wanted it to do.

The downstairs had a finished basement too. Might be a good, dim place for Harper to hang out. She could check it out later.

Cat paused in front of the great room windows and gazed out at the view. Short scrub filled the land between a few swaying pine trees and the expanse of untouched land was simply stunning. There were rocky, snow-capped peaks to the west and long, sweeping hills to the right. Simply magnificent.

The coffee pot gurgled as it finished brewing and she walked back into the kitchen to pour a cup. When Harper roused she would take him a cup. Perhaps.

Cat spent a lazy day on the computer catching up with emails and work while Harper slept. Late in the afternoon he got up and got himself a drink from the refrigerator. Cat watched him gulp the better part of a quart of water, then sit at the kitchen table. The dark glasses were there and he slipped them on to turn and watch the sun go down beyond the mountains.

Cat looked down at her Kindle. It had gone dark because she'd been staring at her husband. Though he'd only been out of the hospital two days she could already tell he was regaining his strength. Even as she watched he pushed to his feet and began to circle the room. Picking up and putting down knick-knacks along the way, he made his way over to her chair. Once he was beside her he rested one of his massive hands on her shoulders, squeezed and moved away. Cat heard him explore the entire house but he didn't go down to the finished basement. Good. She didn't want to try to pick his big butt up off the floor.

Not long after that he headed back to bed.

THE RIDICULOUS PART was he slept most of the next day through as well. Cat kept him fed and when she handed him pills, his antibiotics he assumed, he popped them without a care. It wasn't until evening that he realized that she'd been giving him a light sedative. When he confronted her about it she'd laughed. "On the doctor's orders. I promise. He said that after the drive you needed to relax as much as humanly possible."

Harper had tried to glower at her but it hurt his face. "No more sleeping pills," he ordered. Cat gave him a narrow eyed look but didn't say anything.

Unfortunately, when he wasn't sleeping there wasn't much he could do. The flash of the TV gave him an instant headache, worse than what he'd already had. Cat found a newspaper on the front drive, but he couldn't make his good eye track smoothly enough to read. It had been all he could do to even look at the menu the other night. He tossed the paper to the table in disgust and retreated to his room. The only thing he could do was listen to the music he streamed on his phone.

So he laid down on the bed and covered his head to block out the light and listened to music.

And fell asleep.

Cat woke him for dinner. When he shuffled out, grungy and out of sorts without the arm brace on, she gave him a dirty look but didn't say anything. She offered to cut up his oven-baked chicken, but he waved her away. "I can do it, damn it."

Hands up in entreaty, she left him alone to struggle through the meal.

"That was very good, Cat. Thank you."

He stood up from the chair and left the table, knowing he left a ridiculous, mutilated mess on the plate and table.

Being down was royally pissing him off. He went to bed, determined to have a better day tomorrow.

CAT SHUFFLED TO the coffee maker and pressed the power button, then leaned against the counter to eat a banana. When the coffee was ready she pulled down a ceramic mug from the cupboard and poured a cup. Crossing to the patio doors, she was about to open one when she spotted Harper sitting in one of the lounge chairs under the porch. Retrieving a second mug of coffee she let herself out of the house and crossed to the chair beside him.

The heavy black glasses were on but he turned his head to watch her with his good eye as she set the mug down beside him.

"Thank you, babe."

A shudder rolled through her at the rumbly, sleep-roughened tone of his voice. He'd greeted her just like that many, many mornings over the years. Sometimes he hadn't said a word, just slipped into bed and loved her awake.

It had been everything she could do not to strip off her bra and invite him into bed with her that first night. Her body craved him. But her heart craved him more. It wasn't time for them to take that step yet.

"Did you sleep okay?"

She nodded. "I did. I love seeing the sun coming up out here. The area is beautiful, isn't it?"

"Yes."

She fidgeted with the cup, wishing he'd let her in on what he was thinking. It was a wish she'd made many times over the years. Harper was not a talkative man on a good day, let alone a sleepy morning.

Cat rested her head on the back of the chair and gazed out at the brightening vista. This area of the state was so secluded. Definitely one of the most solitary areas they'd been through. The thought of having no responsibilities other than taking care of Harper and herself for two weeks was quite liberating. She'd had her mother come up from North Carolina to stay with the kids and dog, so she had no worries there. Although the creeping need to cuddle her little man was growing. It was hard just talking to them on the phone.

"Did you sleep okay last night?" she asked him.

"I did, surprisingly. Even though I slept most of the past two days."

"Well, your body is recovering. I wouldn't worry about it. If you need rest, take it."

He sighed deeply and Cat was actually glad to hear it. The bullet that had struck his chest had deflated his left lung, but his respirations were steadily coming back. For days she'd listened to every sound he made in the hospital room.

In her purse she also had a stack of paperwork from the rehab department on things to do to get back to normal. Harper had been through it all before, but it was still nice to have the documentation. This was the first eye injury he'd ever had.

"I don't know if I can stay here for two weeks."

Cat flinched internally at the flat words. "Why not?"

Out of her peripheral vision she could see his hands tighten on the chair arms, the only outward sign he was uncomfortable. She forced herself to stay relaxed.

"Because I need to get back to work. I can't leave LNF short-handed."

"They're not. Duncan said he'd had to hire three people to take your place, but the new guys are already working. Your position is secure, however. I checked with Wilde before I arranged all this."

The information didn't seem to relax him at all. The wood creaked beneath his massive clenching hands.

"Why are you stressing?" she asked calmly.

"I don't know if I can stay here with you that long."

Searing pain shattered her heart at his cold words, but she forced herself to breathe. Icy determination pushed away the pain. "Well, you're going to have to, because this is the last time I'm doing this. This time here at the house is also meant to be for us to decide where this marriage is going, because right now it's circling the drain. I can't hang in this limbo anymore and it's not fair to the kids to expect them to either. So before you bolt out of here just be aware that this is the last time I am going to fight for our marriage."

Unable to stay still any longer, she pushed up out of the chair. "I'm going to go soak in the tub. Or something."

She went through the patio doors, fuming at the ridiculous situation they were in.

CHAPTER FIVE

H ARPER GASPED IN a breath, unable to believe she'd left him gutted that way.

What the fuck?

She'd completely misunderstood him, yet again, because he couldn't make his mouth connect to his brain. This was the most verbal interaction he'd had with anyone in weeks—hell, months maybe.

Choking down a swallow, he searched for the calm center in his being, but she'd just walked out the door. Cat had always been his calm. Even when he wasn't with her just thinking about her slow smile and steady disposition leveled him out. Harper looked down at his hands, unsurprised to see them quake. The thought of not having Cat in his life or even connected to it devastated him.

Resolution filled him. He couldn't let her think he didn't want to be with her.

Shoving up out of the chair he stalked into the house, barely even noticing the twinge in his chest. Cat stood leaning back at the kitchen sink, arms braced on the counter, her head down.

She looked up when he entered and frowned, crossing her arms over her chest in a defensive motion he hadn't seen for a long time.

"You misunderstood me out there," he growled, stalking toward her. "I don't know if I can stay in the same house with you for two weeks and not touch you. And I don't know if touching you would be the wisest decision right now."

She huffed and lifted a sleek black brow at him. "Since when are you the wise one?"

Harper stopped a foot away from her, looking down into her liquid gaze. Had she been about to cry? Her eyes seemed moist. Unable to help himself he reached up to stroke a thumb across her cheekbone. "I'm not the wise one," he admitted. "But I don't want to screw anything up worse than it is."

She gave him a sardonic look. "Things can't get much worse, Harper. And I'm serious about resolving this. Do you know how many excuses I've had to make just to the kids about you? I know you think you're protecting us all, but you're not. We are a family, whether you want to admit it or not."

He shook his head to contradict her, but his equilibrium suddenly spun away from him. Staggering, he reached out where he thought the counter had been, but Cat grabbed him first. Harper let himself lean against her as he fought nausea, his world hurling in circles.

"Oh fuck," he moaned.

Cat tried to hold him up but he pushed her away. "Just let me go. Let me sit down."

She let him go down but she didn't let him go.

Harper landed on his ass hard, but in a way that

helped. It gave him a definite point of reference: the cold tile beneath his ass. He closed his eyes, trying to stabilize. Cat went to her knees in front of him and braced her hands on his shoulders, another point of reference. Dragging in as much air as he could, lungs screaming, he waited for his world to still.

It took a while. Several minutes. Cat merely sat with him, her hands good hard weights on his deltoids. She didn't chatter like a lot of women would. Just stayed there, waiting for him to tell her what he needed.

Harper dared to open his eyes. And though only one eye worked, the world stayed still.

Cat gave him an encouraging smile and sat back on her heels. "Staying solid?"

"Yeah," he sighed.

Fuck, that was irritating. Just standing there talking and his world spun out of control. How the hell was he supposed to lead any kind of productive life if he couldn't have a simple conversation?

"I think between standing up too fast, no food in your stomach and maybe shaking your head you knocked yourself off kilter."

"Fucking ridiculous," he snapped.

Cat started to jerk away but he grabbed her hand. "Not you," he growled. "The situation. I'm so pissed right now."

"You're not used to being anything less than a hundred percent. At all. Your body isn't letting you be in control anymore."

As usual she was right. He could deal with the nausea

and he could probably even deal with the loss of eyesight, but the loss of control pissed him off more than anything.

"Do you think you can get up?"

Without a word he rolled to his feet, forcing himself to act more secure than he actually was. Cat stayed directly in front of him, but his horizon stayed firm. Walking to the kitchen table he sank down into one of the chairs.

"How 'bout I make some breakfast?"

It wasn't really a question because she had already started. Harper watched her putter around the unfamiliar kitchen, opening cupboard drawers to see where everything was. Then she dug in the fridge for a bit, setting ingredients on the marble island.

Harper became a little distracted watching her. This morning she wore a soft t-shirt he didn't recognize and a pair of blue jeans he seemed to remember ripping off her a time or two. His anger faded away as he watched her lean body move. There was no wasted motion with her. It was one of the things that had drawn his eye when he first met her. She hadn't been through the training he had, but she had a natural grace to her that was spellbinding. Cat was competent and controlled in all things, body, mind and spirit.

Even at twenty-two when he'd first met her, he knew he'd been none of those things. His body had been maturing faster than his mind. His spirit had never caught up. The most complete his spirit had ever been had been when he was living with her. All of the fucked up shit he'd grown up with had faded away. There were a couple of brief, shining moments he remembered being completely content with everything in his life. Stupid things like watching her cook him a monster dinner after being deployed for months. Real food made with loving hands after living on government supplied freeze-dried crap made by machines. Playing in the snow on a trip up north, Cat pregnant with Dillon at the time. Watching her tinker under the hood of the truck with him, grease streaked on her cheek.

Cat had been at the center of all of those.

The past year and a half had been hard. Remembering those brilliant moments had kept him moving through his monotonous life.

"I miss watching you," he admitted.

She paused long enough to smile at him, hand propped on her hip. "And I miss feeling the weight of your gaze on me."

Arousal hit him in a rush, causing a different kind of dizziness. That no-holds-barred responsiveness to his overtures had always cranked him up hard. The first moment he'd seen her walking into that restaurant he'd been hit with the most potent arousal he'd ever felt. And over the years as he'd grown to love her, the need had grown as well. Within just a few months they'd been inseparable. If he wasn't on base training, he was with her. The guys in his platoon had thought he was a loner, which was fine because it tied into the sniper mentality, but he was actually just the opposite—home enjoying his wife. He just didn't talk about that part of his life.

Psychologically, Cat had accepted him like no one else ever had. When the miserable excuse he'd had for a father had died when he was twenty-four, it had been a blip on his radar. He'd sent money for the cremation but he hadn't even gone back to Georgia for the service. And nobody had missed him. As the child of an affair, he had never been accepted by either family. Cat had supported his decision to stay away from them all and hadn't said a word to try to sway him otherwise. She knew the kind of abuse he'd lived through.

Because along with that calm-headedness came a knowledge of when to let him run and when to try to rein him in or guide him. Harper knew she played him, but it was all done with their best interests at heart. And she usually manipulated him into doing what he'd wanted to begin with, just hadn't wanted to admit.

Watching her move around the kitchen, he wondered if this was one of those times. Actually, he realized, there were two items he needed to be thinking about. One, was she swaying around the kitchen that way to take his mind off everything else? And two, had she rented this house and arranged this time for them to reconnect because she knew they belonged together, in spite of his issues?

The thought that he might have been wrong for the past year and a half and tortured them both for no reason made his head ache. Hell...

Propping his throbbing head on his hands, he probed at the cuts around his bad eye. Puckered and tender. There were some stitches he'd have to get pulled later. The rest of his head thumped.

"They said that you would be in for some monster headaches."

He slitted his eyes enough to see her set a fresh cup of coffee in front of him and a white pill. Not ibuprofen. "I don't want to be knocked out anymore."

"I know, but if you don't have to have the pain, why not take it? The house is secure. And so are we. We'll get you some breakfast and you can crash."

"Are you going to tuck me in?"

She laughed and paused long enough to toss a grin at him. "Maybe. Although I don't think that would do your headache any good."

"No, but it would take care of the other ache I've got."

Cat gave him a sharp glance, then slowly moved back to the stove. Harper could see the effect he'd had on her though. Those ever-responsive nipples of hers were rock hard. He could see them even through the fabric of her bra and shirt.

And of course, her arousal sharpened his. Daring total destruction, he stood and crossed the room. Amazingly, his head and his feet held steady. Cat looked up when he stopped beside her, but he didn't give her a chance to say anything. Cupping her head in his hands, he pulled her mouth to his.

God...All of the hardships of the past year and a half—hell, the past week—faded away as her lips softened beneath his. Cat accepted his assault like she'd expected it, hoped for it even.

Harper groaned and inhaled her scent, nostalgia stirring as much as the arousal. Their movements were a little awkward at first, but he refused to let that discourage him. Angling his head he requested entrance to the depths of her mouth.

Cat's fists curled into the fabric of his t-shirt and her lips parted, allowing him in. Harper rocked his mouth into hers, nibbling her lush, sweet skin. One hand slid down to hold her arm at the elbow.

The nice thing about Cat was that he didn't have to bend in half to kiss her. At six foot five that really meant a lot. She was a tall woman, lean almost to the point of skinny. But she had curves in all the right places. Harper let his hands drift down her waist and they ended up cupping her ass.

They both paused as he squeezed and he knew she was wondering if he would pick her up like he used to. Pulling her tight, he tested the pain in his chest. Manageable. Probably wouldn't hurt too bad.

"Don't."

Damn, she was a freaking mind reader. Smiling against her mouth, he pulled away to grab a breath. "You were remembering too, weren't you?"

The wash of color under her pale cheeks and her dilated pupils spoke volumes. "Hard not to. You used to haul my ass everywhere."

Harper grinned, remembering. Hell, he used to have her hop on his back for him to train with, her weight and balance perfect.

Before he could lean in again she pulled away and

crossed back to the sink. "I think it's a little early to get physical. You're still healing."

"Fuck that. We've made love when I was worse off before. Seems like I remember a visit late at night at Walter Reed."

Her cheeks pinkened before she turned away. "That was different."

Chuckling, he decided to let her have her freedom. She could stew on her arousal; then the next time he approached her she would be more receptive. There were some things he needed to do anyway. With a final regretful glance he left the kitchen and walked to the small office he'd found, dropping into the leather office chair. The living room was more comfortable but it had a huge expanse of windows looking out over the landscape. Way too bright.

Duncan didn't answer his cell phone, which was probably smart. Harper had some words for him that wouldn't be particularly nice. His boss had sold him out without a word of warning. Although was being with Cat actually a hardship?

Chad picked up on the first ring. "Hey, Harper! How's it hanging, buddy?"

Snorting in spite of himself, he swung around to the desk. "Surprisingly well, Lowell. I would have appreciated a heads up, though."

Chad laughed on the other end of the line. "About what? Oh, the kidnapping? She was doing exactly what we've wanted to do for a long time. She just managed to do it with a little more ease. You've needed a break for a while, dude. When's the last time you took a day of vacation?"

He never had. They both knew that.

"Cat made a good case for your abduction and we agreed with her reasoning. I think you guys need to work on some personal stuff anyway." A wrapper crinkled on the other end of the line as Lowell put something in his mouth. "Mercy said to tell you hi next time I talked to you and that she thanks you for sending her bear back."

Damn. Cat must have done that too. She'd been a busy woman the last couple of days.

"Tell her I appreciated the loan."

"I will. Enjoy yourself, buddy. The company can run without you for a while. Get your marriage in order. A few months ago I wouldn't have understood how important that is, but I do now. If she's the one for you you need to invest time in her."

Harper knew he was right; it was just hard taking a step back. Daring to go out on a limb, he cleared his throat. "I left because of the anxiety and the paranoia. I thought I was going to hurt someone."

Silence stretched for several seconds. "But if you leave the good because you're worried about the bad, the bad wins, right? You have a better chance of getting right in the head if you have the right foundation at home."

Harper sighed. Though he had a few years on his boss age-wise the guy had the right of it. "Yeah, I know what you're saying is sound—it's just hard. The worries are persistent."

"I know, but I also know you're more persistent.

You're a damn bull. You need to find a way to keep your family together."

There was work to be done. Harper hung up feeling more secure in himself and his situation.

They needed to work on their marriage. Cat was completely right about that. And maybe he just had to have the faith in them to commit to it.

Next he made a quick call to Gunny.

"Mr. Preston. How the fuck are you?"

Harper smirked at the greeting. "Fine, Palmer. But I'm feeling a little exposed. Think you can send me some things?"

Within a few minutes he had the security of the house mapped out and John promised to overnight him a box of equipment. If he was going to stay here for two weeks he needed to feel more secure.

CAT BRACED HERSELF against the counter and dragged in a heavy breath. The man was so damn sexy. He didn't even have to try very hard to point out how hard up she was. It had been a year and a half since he'd left and she'd felt every day of it.

Even beat up and bruised he appealed to her. Maybe even more so because she wanted to mother him.

The man didn't need a mother though. He needed a wife with direction. And she was definitely that person. Cat was bound and determined to drag him home. Even if home needed to be in Colorado with his new job, she didn't care as long as they were all together. She could do web design anywhere as long as she had her computer. And the kids would do just about anything to see him and be with him again.

Dillon worried her. So impressionable right now, she had truly been daddy's girl. Cat knew that her daughter had taken on part of the guilt of her father leaving, and it couldn't continue. She had too many other things she needed to be thinking about—boys and grades and what position she wanted to play in softball. The worry in her young, stormy grey eyes so like her father's had aged her. They'd aged Cat as well because she felt helpless to eradicate those worries.

As for Tate...well, he kept bouncing along. But he had been asking about his father less and less. That brought the tears at night. In the depths of the silence of the house when no one needed her she let herself cry. That was the only time she allowed herself to weaken.

Turning back to the stove she stirred the eggs.

CHAPTER SIX

THEY HAD A quiet day, each occupied with their own thoughts. It was comforting being around each other. Just knowing that Harper was in the house was a huge present to Cat. Every time she thought about him being down the hallway or on the deck a little thrill went through her belly. Like Christmas was just around the corner. She basked in those warm feelings.

There was also a taunting thrill of desire. All day they were aware of each other—every little cough or move. At one point Harper stood looking out the living room's huge bay window and Cat just had to stop and stare. The man was massive; broad shoulders cocked as he leaned against the window casement, tight waist leading to lean hips and long legs. He had one of the nicest asses she'd ever seen on a man. Cat had to force herself to turn away before she walked up behind him and wrapped her arms around that lean waist, then tugged him into the bedroom.

Dinner was a quiet affair. Harper ate with an actual appetite, piling away the spaghetti and garlic bread like he used to do. Cat found herself watching him chew and swallow, heavy Adam's apple bouncing. She could still see his chest bandage beneath the cotton of his t-shirt.

They probably ought to look at it later to make sure everything was healing.

"Are you still designing?" he asked abruptly.

"I am. I brought my computer with me so I can work."

A lot had changed in the eighteen months he'd been gone. She'd worked like a dog to make her business truly profitable enough that they didn't need his income. If he decided to divorce her tomorrow she wouldn't be left floundering for a way to take care of her kids. Was she making a lot of money? No. But enough that they could live on.

Right now the money he direct deposited into their joint account was used for incidentals. Kids' clothes, extras. And her money was used to run the household. Inside she was incredibly proud of that fact. It was paying for their time here in the house.

When she and Harper had gotten together they'd clicked immediately. They'd been set up by one of her girlfriends who at the time had been dating one of Harper's teammates. Harper had already graduated BUDs and been assigned to Team 8. Cat remembered seeing him walk into the restaurant in Norfolk, tall and imposing, naturally intimidating, and her heart had raced. She'd known that night that he was going to be the love of her life.

Harper had fallen fast too. When they'd first started dating he'd been brash and cocky, smiling all the time, but leery of her affections. As a child he'd been an afterthought. If his alcoholic parents were around they'd toss him something to eat, but for the most part he'd had to take care of himself. Cat had been brought up in a loving, accepting environment, totally different than his. They'd had some serious adjustments to make with each other, but it had worked out.

Within a few months they'd eloped. A few months later she was pregnant with Dillon and he was out of the country shooting bad guys. For probably seventy-five percent of their married life they had been apart.

Boy, that twenty-five percent really made up for the rest, though.

"I'm glad you didn't give that up," he told her softly. "It really seems to feed your soul."

"It does," she agreed.

Cat had always been artistic. She'd gone to college for design but once she'd married Harper her plans had changed. Drastically. When she'd gotten pregnant they had both agreed that it would be better for her to stay home while the baby was small. And she didn't regret one minute of that time in her life.

Was it the third time he'd been deployed when she'd decided to go back to school and finish her degree? She couldn't remember exactly. By the time Dillon was about five Cat was back in school part time. She'd started college at the same time her daughter had started pre-school. Luckily, by that time they'd had a lot of support from the other team members' wives and families. Cat had traded babysitting with a couple of the other mothers on base and it had worked out surprisingly well.

Now she ran her own business.

"It's grown," she told him. "I now have a handful of monthly customers and several on the schedule for the next year. You might be surprised how well I'm doing."

Harper looked at her, brows raised. He let them drop almost immediately, though. It must have hurt. "That's awesome, Cat. Really. I know I was gone a large part of our marriage and I worried about you getting bored."

She frowned. "I didn't get bored, necessarily. I had the kids. But I needed something to fulfill the creative side of me."

Harper sat back in the chair and shifted his chest a little, looking like he was uncomfortable. "I always worried that you would find another man to take better care of you. You're a good-looking woman and I wouldn't have blamed you. The wife of a SEAL is not an easy job."

The quiet words held brutal honesty.

"I wouldn't have cheated on you. I had opportunities definitely, but that's not the kind of person I am."

Harper smiled and looked down at his lap.

"What?" she asked.

His hard silver-grey eyes flicked up to her face, seeming to glow. "Is it wrong that I like knowing men wanted you?"

Cat shook her head, laughing. "Really? I profess my commitment to our marriage and you get jacked knowing men were after me?"

Harper made a face, looking sheepish. "What can I say? You've always turned me on but there's something about having what another man wants that satisfies the competitive caveman in me."

By the pleasure curling in her stomach it apparently satisfied something in her as well. The desire she had banked all day returned.

Cat played with her half empty water glass, swirling the base in the moisture on the table. "It always made me excited when I saw women looking at you as well," she admitted. "But I worried when you weren't around."

Harper narrowed his eyes and leaned forward, invading her personal space. "I never cheated. Ever. Were there opportunities? Of course. But I was never tempted. Most of the women that hit on me I couldn't even stand to listen to."

Some knot of tangled emotion eased in her chest. Harper was a virile man. He had a healthy sex drive. When they'd been together they'd loved almost every day. But in the back of her mind had been the fear that he'd sated those drives with someone else. Tears smarted her eyes as the relief flowed through her. She looked down at her plate, unwilling to let him see.

Hard fingers tilted her face up. Anger sparked in his silver eyes. "I would never cheat on you. I take my marriage vows seriously. I always have."

She nodded and a tear dripped down her cheek. "I know you have but a year and a half is a really long time. Longer than any of your deployments. I guess I kind of expected...well, I wouldn't have blamed you if you had."

"But I would have blamed me and that's not something I need on my conscience, not along with everything else," he told her firmly. "Besides, I've never been drawn to anyone else since I met you. Did I tell you you look beautiful today? Because you do."

With that massive, easy strength of his he reached for the base of her chair and slid her around the table until she sat directly in front of him. Then, cupping her face, he kissed her.

This time there was no awkwardness. Just calm, steady, sweet affection like they used to have. Cat wrapped her arms around his neck, one hand brushing the stubbly hair on the back of his head. With a little urging from his fingers she shifted into his lap, even as their lips stayed fused.

Cat knew that sleeping with her husband right now could potentially muddy the situation they were in, but her body refused to listen. It had been so long since she'd been loved. So long since she'd been held. Her body ached with need for him.

Harper stood with her in his arms, then set her on her feet. With one hand he tugged her along behind him to the bedroom she was using. Harper urged her down onto the bed but immediately covered her body with his own. There was a twinge on his face as he braced his body over top of hers until he shifted most of his weight to the right arm, smiling down at her. "You have about three seconds to tell me how bad of an idea this is, then I'm going to fuck you like I've been dreaming of for the past year and a half."

Cat's eyes fluttered shut as a rolling wave of arousal moved through her body. He was right. She *should* say something, but her mind was completely blank. Shaking her head, she cupped his face in her hands again, tilting her mouth up to his. Harper accommodated her immediately, pressing his mouth into hers so hard she knew her lips would be bruised later. But she didn't care. Her warrior was finally back in her arms.

Harper ground his hips into her pelvis, erection straining. Cat widened her knees and arched upward. He growled in her ear, pressing hard, nibbling kisses down the length of her neck. Goosebumps erupted all over her skin.

He pulled away enough to stand beside the bed. Cat heard the zipper of his jeans rasp down, then the shuffle of pants dropped to the floor. The window blinds above the bed were wide open letting in the evening light and for the first time in too long, she got to see him fully naked. God, he was gorgeous. Even after being bedbound for the past week and a half his tan skin glowed with vitality. Black and gray tattoos decorated his heavy shoulders and forearms. The design on his right pectoral of the *loyalty and courage* tattoo stirred nostalgia. It had been one of the first he'd gotten and she had helped design it. She ran her fingers over it as he came over top of her again, wondering if he'd ever regretted getting it done.

The left side of his chest was clear of ink. "It's a good thing you didn't have anything put here." She brushed her fingers over the bright white bandage covering his gunshot wound.

He grinned down at her. "I had an appointment set up for three days ago to get a piece put there."

Cat laughed and pressed a kiss to his strong chin. "It always works out the way it needs to, huh? That would have been a mess to try to fix. You need to quit getting shot."

Harper nodded and kissed her again, grinding his pelvis into her. Cat huffed out a breath, knowing that their coming together was a done thing now. They'd always laughed and loved, moving seamlessly from one emotion to the next. Ebbing and flowing like the tide. "I've missed this, Harper."

He nuzzled her ear, going still as he inhaled against her. "I have too. More than you could possibly know."

Emotion choked her, making her hands tremble as they wrapped around his shoulders. Many, many nights she had cradled him in her arms just like this. In the dark of the night when he didn't have to put on a front for the world, he would let her be the strong one, protecting him from the unrelenting memories. Though he hadn't told her a great deal, Cat knew that as a sniper for the SEALs he had done brutal things. Things that would rock her core as a person, but that he had been charged to do as a weapon for the US government.

She'd seen the haunted look in his eyes when he looked at the kids sometimes, as if he wanted to hold them against the world forever. There were a couple of times she'd felt like that as well, but for completely different reasons. Her kids were growing so fast. If they didn't straighten out their home lives now they would have severe issues when they were grown.

None of that mattered though as she ran her hands

up his arms and across his massive shoulders. Harper had always been a big, strapping man, but he had bulked up since she'd seen him last. His biceps strained as he loomed over her but there was no quiver. His strength had begun to return.

Harper pulled back enough to strip off her jeans and the string bikinis. Cat removed her own t-shirt and bra, flinging them to the side of the bed. Fresh moisture flooded her as she took in the masculine strength of him. Even as she watched Harper fisted himself and pumped, then crawled over top of her again. Cat's eyes burned from not blinking, but she didn't want to miss—or forget—anything that was about to happen.

The head of his cock rested against the opening to her body but didn't penetrate. Instead Harper worked himself up and down, from the wellspring of her body to the trigger of her release. Cat jerked as he rocked over her clit, shifting him to the side that she liked. As she looked down the long line of his torso, down the dark trail of hair leading to his groin to watch the length of him about to slide into her, she shuddered. It was too much to bear.

Then, with one long surge, he sank into her.

Cat moaned at being fulfilled for the first time in so long. Breathing deeply, she waited for her body to remember Harper. He seemed to be absorbing the feel of them together again as well. Faint tremors shook his body, as if he were already too close to the edge.

"Are you okay?" she whispered, concerned that it was going to be too much for his injuries.

In answer he pressed a kiss to her temple. "I am. Just trying not to come. It's been a long time for me."

Cat grinned up at him and he leaned in for another kiss. "It's been a long time for both of us."

She rocked up into him to encourage him to move. Groaning, he pushed in, then for the barest minute stilled again, but the compulsion to move proved to be too strong. Harper began picking up the pace.

Cat gasped at the feeling of his body plunging deep into hers. He was much larger than average and it had taken a long time to get used to the feel of him pounding into her. The advantage to that size was that he rubbed against her G-spot constantly. She was so sexed up for him that it was only a few heavy strokes before she was dancing on the edge of bliss. Harper felt and recognized her quivers because he paused to let them catch a breath. Cat wanted to weep with frustration. Holding him in her arms was so emotional for her; then he wrung out her emotions even harder by denying her release.

Harper kissed her, arching into her in a single stroke, just enough to take her back to that edge. Then he paused to let her tumble back down from that point.

Tears were dripping down the corners of her eyes and into her hair by the time he began to move steadily inside her, building momentum. But the release he had denied her was that much sharper when she did reach it. Cat screamed as one of the most cataclysmic orgasms she'd ever felt crashed over her, sending her body thrashing, trying to get away from the relentless power stroking between her thighs. But Harper was a man possessed. As she arched beneath him he seized his own release, hard hands gripping her hips to take every bit of him. His movements suddenly stalled out and his face darkened with furious, jaw-slackening pleasure. With a series of furious, sharp thrusts he cried out his release.

Cat either blacked out or dozed off for a few minutes. When she woke her body still rippled with the occasional aftershock. Harper had propped himself over top of her, head resting against the mattress. Their breathing had begun to regulate but they were still sweaty. She dragged in oxygen, resting her hands on his flanks. Harper moved just enough to pull out of her and lay to her side. Cat rocked her head to look at him in the dimness of the room but he had already dozed off.

If the man hadn't been shot ten days ago she probably would have been a little put out. They'd just had mind-blowing sex for the first time since their separation. She felt like they needed to celebrate.

But she would let him sleep.

Cat slipped out of the bed, moving stealthily enough to flip a sheet over Harper's form curled on his side, snoring softly. Feeling daring, she ran her fingers through his short hair, covered his shoulder and headed to the shower.

It had been a long time since her body had felt this way. As she stepped under the water and lathered she took note of all the sensitive places. The stubble on his jaw had chafed her chin and cheeks, his hands had bruised her hips a bit. But it was all done in the heat of passion and love. She loved feeling like this. The other half of her heart was sleeping out there on the bed.

As she left the bathroom she took care to move quietly when she slipped between the sheets. It was still fairly early for her, but what the hell. It had been such a long time since she'd had the chance to sleep with her husband. Harper didn't move. Feeling daring, Cat backed her ass into the curve of his lap. Immediately his heavy arm wrapped around her hips and pulled her back into him. Sighing, she savored the feel of his heat as long as she could before she let sleep overcome her.

CHAPTER SEVEN

ARPER WOKE STIFF all over and sore. Blinking, he reached up to rub the sleep from his eyes and cursed. Fuck, he'd forgotten. His right eye and the skin around it throbbed where he'd rubbed his hands. How could he have forgotten about it?

Cat shifted beside him, moaning as she rolled onto her back. The sheet slipped down and her breast peeked out. With a groan of appreciation he reached over and ran a fingertip over her nipple. The pain from rubbing his eye was almost immediately forgotten.

Before she even opened her eyes Cat smiled and stretched her arms above her head. Her second breast popped out from beneath the covers.

Harper groaned at the sight of her, flushed and swollen from sleep but so naturally sexy it made his mouth water. With no reservation she rolled toward him, gave him a big kiss then rolled out of bed to pad to the bathroom. Harper watched her go and was once again grateful for his single damn eye. The thought of never seeing her luscious ass and the long line of her back again devastated him.

When she came out of the bathroom, lean hips swaying and crawled across the bed to straddle his hips,

Harper thought he'd died and gone to heaven. Though it hurt his face he grinned up at her. "Good morning."

"Good morning." She leaned forward to press a kiss to his lips. "Did you have a good sleep?"

"You know," he said thoughtfully, "I did. I think I must have had sexy dreams though."

He arched his hips up into her enough that she could feel the erection under the sheet at his waist.

Cat grinned and burrowed her hand beneath the sheet, wrapping her fingers around his dick. "Why yes, I believe you did. Lucky for you though, I did too. I planned on jumping your bones again whether you were awake or not."

Harper laughed, loving her all the more for being playful. "Well, that's a good way to wake me up."

She nodded and wiggled an eyebrow. "I know. I remember, dear."

Leaning away she tugged the sheet from his hips, exposing his erection to the cool of the room. Having her gaze on him hardened him even further, but before he could say anything she had lifted her hips and stood him straight up with her fingertips. Harper took a great breath of air as her wild heat settled down over top of him.

Cat swiveled her hips, snugging down tight. She was deliciously wet. That wetness was a woman's proof of desire. The undeniable evidence that she wanted *him*.

He had dreamt of her, over and over again. Perhaps she had been dreaming about him as well.

Cat had a natural athleticism that kept her lean and

flexible. Her thighs strained as she hovered over top of him and started to move up and down. Her pace wasn't hurried and he had to laugh because it was a little obvious he was an afterthought. Cat knew how to pleasure herself and she made no bones about doing it now. Just as she had many times through the years they'd been married.

Bracing his hips up from the mattress, Harper encouraged her to move harder, the next level up in her search for release. Cat moaned and brought herself down on him more aggressively, faster, eyes closed, breasts bouncing.

Reaching up he tweaked her nipples, making her cry out. When she switched to doing a heavy grind Harper knew she was close. Cupping her hips in his palms he pulled her tighter against him, bracing himself up off the mattress. Cat started to pant. Her hands slapped onto his wrists, squeezing as her body started to tighten around his. Harper didn't plan on coming with her but as she started to keen high in her throat and spasm around his cock, his body surged to join her.

Cat was beautiful in her orgasm, lean body flushed with color, clutching and releasing his. Harper enjoyed his orgasm as well, but there was something precious in just watching her. The way she moved brought back many nights of loving, and it brought home how many nights he had missed.

Cat melted to his chest, her breathing raspy. Though it hurt his chest a little to have her there, he refused to push her away. Instead he reached up and cradled her to him, pressing kisses to her brow. "You are stunning," he whispered.

She shifted a little, enough to press a kiss to his chin. "You're tasty. As soon as I saw you sleeping beside me I wanted you again."

"Hm," he agreed. "If I had seen you first we would still be in this position."

She giggled. "Those damn sexy dreams. Sent to bedevil us." She gasped with laughter. "Oh, wait. Not bedeviled. Maybe pickled."

Harper laughed out loud. "You got pickled and I'm being bedeviled."

He danced his fingers up her sides, sending her into even more laughter.

It was so nostalgic, loving and laughing together. His throat tightened with emotion as he watched her wipe tears from her eyes.

Cat seemed to sense the shift in him to serious because she slid from his chest to sit beside him. Harper folded an arm beneath his head and looked up at her, trying to memorize her face. It was a useless exercise though because he already had. All her emotions, the way her right eyebrow had a little point of hair in the middle, the way she gasped when she was truly enjoying herself. There was no way he could escape the memory of any of it. And he certainly didn't want to.

But was he open to accepting her into his life again?

"You slept like a rock last night."

Harper blinked. That hadn't been what he'd been expecting. "Did you drug me?"

Her eyes widened and her mouth fell open with indignation. "No, I didn't drug you! I slept with you. And you," she paused to point a finger in his direction, "didn't dream. I woke several times and you were still sleeping like a rock. No moaning, no shouting, no jumping out of bed to attack shadows or pace. No reaching out to stroke your gun on the bedside table."

Harper frowned at her description of how he used to be. "I think I'm still recovering."

She lifted a brow at the sidestep. "So, you're telling me you're just as bad as you used to be?"

He looked up at the ceiling. "No, I'm not as bad as when I first left the Team, but I still have the nagging worries and dreams."

"Night terrors or dreams?"

Rolling up in bed he swung his legs to the side, planting his feet. "I still have occasional night terrors but not like I used to. Duncan makes a counselor available to us and I've gone to her several times," he admitted. "For the past year, actually."

Cat didn't say anything so he glanced over his shoulder at her. She sat naked and open with tears glittering in her eyes. "I wanted you to go to counseling when you left the house but you said you didn't need it."

Harper hated to see the hurt in her expression. She *had* urged him to go to the counselors but it hadn't been until his life had fallen apart and he'd had to leave his family that he'd realized how critical it was. "I know." Reaching out with his good arm, he tugged her around to face him. "But it wasn't until I was faced with the possibility of never seeing you again that I realized I had to make some changes. And it's not something a guy like me wanted to admit, you know?"

She swiped her fingers under her eyes, catching tears before they fell. "I'm very happy that you stepped up like that."

"Once I got to hanging with the rest of the guys at LNF and they started to talk about their own counseling it became easier for me to think about doing it."

"You're not less of a man because of it," she told him firmly. "The exact opposite, actually. I think you're more of a man for doing it."

Harper didn't say anything, just wrapped his arms around her and pressed a kiss to her head.

After a few minutes Cat pulled back enough to look up at him. "I'm going to go shower again. Would you like to join me?"

Nodding, he helped her untangle herself from the sheets and followed along as she walked into the bathroom.

"I WANT TO go for a hike."

Harper gave her a frown but didn't try to argue with her. "Where to?"

Cat motioned toward the back yard. "There's a path that climbs the ridge. I'd like to head in that direction. Do you feel up to it?"

Harper nodded and Cat knew he wouldn't have dared give her any other answer. He was too hard-headed to tell her he wasn't up to it.

She had to admit, though, he was getting stronger. Out of the hospital for four days now his strength had definitely begun to return. He ate everything she cooked and snacked in between if he wanted to. The dizzy spell he'd had the second day hadn't bothered him again.

Cat grabbed a light jacket to stave off the chill of the morning and let herself out the door to the back deck. Harper followed right behind her, latching the door closed behind him. The house was now locked up tight and she had the key in her pocket.

As she stepped down onto the frosty ground she tried not to watch Harper too closely. If he wavered or stumbled she could slip in beside him and wrap her arm around his waist.

"Quit worrying, Cat."

Clenching her jaw, she marched forward and up through the slight border of brush around the yard. Little scrub trees crowded around her legs, but she aimed for the trail she could see winding up the incline. A rabbit darted a little ways away and she felt Harper jerk behind her. "Just a rabbit."

"I know," he grumbled. "It was on my right though and I didn't see it right away."

Frowning, she didn't say anything, but she felt like crap. If she could help him get used to being sightless on that side she absolutely would.

They tromped up the hill for the better part of thirty minutes and finally drew up on the crest of the ridge. Sighing, Cat found a rocky outcropping to sit on to gaze at the view. "Wow," she sighed. Shifting over, she made sure Harper had a place to sit as well.

The ridge they had just climbed was small compared to the one in front of them. If they continued east the trail snaked its way to the top of that ridge as well, with the Rocky Mountains beyond, but Cat had no intentions of going any farther. Though he hadn't said a word she knew Harper had to be worn out. She handed him a bottle of water from the little shoulder sack she wore. Twisting off the cap, he chugged most of it down.

They were in a bit of a strange place emotionally. Though they'd made love—or was it sex?—they were each still too protected to reach out and be like they used to be. Cat knew she didn't want her heart broken again, so she was a little scared to hope. They hadn't talked about what was going to happen when their two weeks were up. That was another cliff they were dancing the edge of, unsure which way to go. Cat loved her husband but they needed to get some things settled.

"It was one of the hardest things I've ever done, leaving you alone in Virginia."

She glanced at him out of the corner of her eye, wondering why he had brought that subject up. "For a while it just felt like another deployment. The hardest part was not talking to you. I mean, even when you were in the field you were able to get to a phone occasionally. The complete shutdown was hard. You sent me that note a couple months after you left and I read that damn thing over and over again, trying to get some idea of what was going through your mind. I was so worried that you were going to hurt yourself. And the return address was a total dead-end. I tried to track you through that."

He shook his head. "It was just a post office I stopped at on the way to Colorado for the job with Duncan. I didn't plan on staying."

Something occurred to her then. "When did you apply for the job with Duncan?"

He heaved a heavy sigh and she had a feeling she wasn't going to like the answer. "I had started putting out feelers about a few months after I left the Teams, but I didn't hear anything for a good while. When he called for an interview I jumped at the chance."

Cat frowned at the flat words. He'd jumped at the chance to get away from them.

"You couldn't even acknowledge the fact that you needed counseling but you applied to his company, which seems to only hire disabled vets."

Harper winced. "Yeah. I know. This sounds a little crazy but I think in the back of my mind I knew I needed counseling. I just didn't want to admit it. And being with the Teams it's hard to admit to that stuff. Going to work for a company that requires it kind of gave me a pass. Hell, I don't know."

Cat could see that. Harper was one of the most stubborn men she knew. Incredibly masculine, borderline overbearing. She could see where admitting he needed help would chafe.

"And I knew Wilde from years ago," he continued. "He'd given us support on an op that went to hell. We weren't under his command but we'd worked together. I think it helped that he'd remembered my Team."

"Well," she said softly. "Regardless of why you got counseling, at least you got it. Are you still going?"

He nodded, crossing his long legs in front of him. "I have a standing appointment with Dr. Singh every other week."

"And have you talked to him about us?" she asked, breath held.

"Dr. Singh is a her, and yes, I've told her about you."

When he stopped there Cat could have screamed in frustration. "And?"

He turned his head to look at her with his good eye. "And she doesn't agree with the fact that I left you behind. But she's too nice of a lady to call me an outright bastard." He heaved a great sigh and pivoted toward her a little on the rock. "I know you don't agree with my decision to leave, but it made me feel better about the safety of my family. All of the things I was paranoid about I could control if I was away from you guys. I didn't have to worry about somebody trying to attack me and you becoming collateral damage. Or the kids. God. I had a huge bounty on my head and it literally felt like a target on my back. And then there was that fucking day when I woke up and Tate had my gun. It would have gutted me if he had pulled the trigger that morning. You know? I would have taken that bullet happily, because it was my fault. If anything had happened to you, my world would have ended."

She saw the glitter of tears in his eyes before he turned to look out over the vista.

Cat wiped her own eyes, but felt like there was some softening in his stance to stay away. "I feel the same way, Harper. That morning was one of the worst of my life. Luckily Tate doesn't even remember the incident." She reached out and rubbed a hand over his broad back. "But when I married you I knew there was a chance that something could happen. Did I expect a normal life? Hell, no. You were a Navy SEAL, one of the most elite fighting machines in the country. I knew when the government called you were gone." She choked out a laugh. "What woman would sign up for that craziness?" She heaved a great sigh and leaned against his back. "A woman who loved her fierce, dedicated warrior and knew his country would always take precedence over his family."

He shifted as if to argue but she rocked her head against him. "But the problem is, even after you left it was still taking precedence. I know you were worried about retribution because of what you had done over there, but the chances of that actually happening are so slim. And I realize that going from running a million miles a minute, saving people, shooting guns to suburban home life is a devastating change. I had hoped that the training job would be a good transition between the two, but it didn't seem to even have a bearing."

"It did have a bearing," he disagreed. "I had started to slow down. But you're right. It's so hard turning off the war machine. Over there you expect to be shot at. You expect to lose your best friends. When you sit in the dirt to talk to a guy and watch his head explode in front of you, it's hard not to be that way."

Tears flooded her eyes and ran down her cheeks at the harsh visual, but Harper just breathed through it. Cat tightened her arms around his back, hoping her presence could help him in some small way. "I'm sorry."

He turned to look at her. "I'm not telling you this for sympathy. I just wanted you to understand how drastically different our lives were. I had to find a way to adapt to all those changes. Dr. Singh is helping me do that. And I'm beginning to see the light at the end of the tunnel."

He leaned forward and pressed a kiss to her forehead. "I'm amazed at all you've had to put up with and humbled that you're willing to put up with more. For a while there I wondered if just letting you go wouldn't be better for everyone."

"It wouldn't," she murmured, resting her head against his chest. "You are a part of us. We can't let you go like that."

His heart thudded beneath her ear and his arms tightened around her but he didn't say anything more. She didn't need him to. Just the fact that he'd opened up to her so much was incredible. He'd never done that before. At least not without the situation falling into a screaming match.

Harper jostled her a little. "Come on, there's something I want to show you."

He pushed up from the rock then gave her a hand up. Cat picked up her sack and began to follow as he started down the trail, away from the house. "Wait a minute. What do you mean you have something to show me? How do you know where you're going, Harper?"

Grinning at her over his shoulder, he didn't pause. "I may have reconnoitered a little."

Cat felt her mouth drop open in shock and she stopped dead on the trail. "You did what? You just got out of the hospital. You went hiking? When?"

Harper kept moving but she jogged ahead of him, holding a hand out to stop him. "Answer me, damn it!"

Harper paused, jaw clenched. "I went out the second day. Not too far. And I've been solid on my feet for a while now."

Cat looked at him, aghast. "You weren't solid the second day we were here. That was the day you fell on your ass in the kitchen. What would have happened if you'd tripped on a damn rock out here or something? I never would have found you."

Anger sparked in his eyes. "That was a chance I was willing to take," he snapped. "I had to make sure we were safe here."

Cat rocked back on her heels, surprised that he'd snapped at her, as if she were the one in the wrong. But when she looked at his expression, he seemed to realize that he'd been in the wrong.

He just hadn't been able to help himself.

Her anger cooled. As a SEAL he was used to pushing himself beyond everything. If she were honest with herself she was a little surprised he hadn't gone out the first night after she had gone to bed. That was just the kind of guy he was.

Anytime they went on a family trip he would scout

out the area. And as a sniper he always went for the high ground—rooftops, fire towers. He had taken her word for their surroundings at the hospital, but she should have known he wouldn't be content with that forever.

It was why he'd had to mount the little cameras and motion detectors that had arrived this morning from his boss in Denver. There were wires running along the floor of the house and into the den because she wouldn't let him drill holes in the walls. *It's a damn rental house, for shit's sake*, she'd told him.

Suddenly the anger just drained out of her. If they were going to put this marriage back together they needed to let all this little stuff go. Harper was fine—that was the main thing. "If you go out again, at least tell me. That way I'm not looking for you in places you aren't. Okay?"

Harper nodded and seemed a little surprised she was letting it go. "I will. I promise. And I didn't do it to piss you off. I just..." his voice trailed away. He looked out over the ridge as if he could see insurgents sweeping over it, then back to her. "I need to know we are secure."

She nodded and walked forward to hook her elbow through his arm. "Okay, Harper. So what did you find?"

CHAPTER EIGHT

H E STARTED WALKING again, navigating around larger rocks. They walked down a short slope then had to go single file. Cat couldn't tell what he was following, but she made sure to step where he did. They walked like that, kind of sideways on the hill, for about ten minutes before he finally slowed. There were bigger rocks here, reddish, that they had to weave around. Suddenly he paused and stepped to the side so she could see around him.

Cat gasped and walked forward, fascinated. The little spring seeping up from the rocky ground was an oasis. It was no bigger than a puddle really, but grass and bushes had crowded around it. "How on earth did you find this?" she whispered.

Harper grinned at her. "I followed the trail we were just on and it led me here."

She frowned at him, not understanding. "What trail? I thought we were just walking."

He shook his head, then suddenly reached out for a rock to steady himself. But he didn't go down this time. After a few deep breaths he blinked at her. "We've been following small animal trails for the past fifteen minutes. I noticed them when I was scouting the area the other night. There were so many heading in this direction I knew there had to be something close."

Cat shook her head, amazed and exasperated. There had been no trail that she'd seen, just rocky, sandy ground. She snorted. Leave it to the SEAL to find the only movement in the area. And the only water.

Circling the spring she tried to see the trails. There were a few faint lines through the underbrush, but that was it. She never would have seen them if he hadn't pointed them out.

Harper knelt down, swirling his fingers through the clear water. Cupping his hand, he raised a handful to his mouth and swallowed. Then, groaning, he drank more.

Frowning, she shook her head. "Aren't you worried about getting a nasty belly bug from that?"

Laughing, he looked up at her, water dripping off his chin. "If you had ever seen some of the places we've drunk from before, you wouldn't worry about this little spring."

Though his words didn't relax her completely they did take some starch out of her spine. The chances of getting something nasty were probably infinitesimal, but that didn't mean she was going to do that.

Cat took a swig of water from her bottle, then found a patch of dirt to sit on that wasn't too rocky. Harper finished drinking and swiped some water up over his head. It wasn't particularly hot, but he was sweating a bit. He plopped down beside her in the dirt.

"Thanks for not freaking out too bad."

Cat sighed, knowing she'd always been a little tight

around him. "I never meant to make you feel defensive about what you did. I've just always been used to being the one in charge. The kids listen to me."

"I'm not the kids."

She snorted. "I know that. But it's a control thing. When you weren't there I kept control. Sometimes even when you were there I kept control."

Harper picked up a rock, turning it in his hand. "When I came back a lot of the time I didn't want anything to do with being in charge. I'd been in charge of a lot of lives over there. When I came home it was nice not to be responsible for all that. Not to be responsible for anything."

Cat could understand that. Maybe someday she'd be able to relinquish a little control.

"Look there."

Cat followed the line of Harper's broad finger pointing down at the climbing slope across from them. She didn't see anything at first, then something moved. It took her eyes several seconds to focus on the rabbit hopping through the underbrush. The thing was a long ways away and she was amazed Harper had seen it. "I can't believe you spotted that. It has to be the better part of a half-mile away."

Looking down at her, he grinned, and she knew he had just realized how far away it was as well. "Come on. I'm getting hungry."

They hiked back to the house. Cat was tired, energized, but felt a little grungy. "I may go take a shower."

Harper nodded, crossing to dig in the refrigerator.

He dug out a couple of packages, then grabbed the bread from the counter. "PT gave you paperwork, right? Anything in there about strengthening this eye?"

Cat frowned. "I'm not sure. The packet is still in my purse. You can get it."

It wasn't until she was soaped up and completely lathered before she remembered what else was in her purse.

Oh, fuck!

Cat hurried through her shower, rinsing off in record time. She bundled the towel around her, fear making her movements uncoordinated. If he had found the other she needed to be there to explain.

She jerked a pair of sweats on and a T-shirt, her skin still beaded with moisture. She was running her fingers through her short hair when she entered the den. Harper sat in one of the padded chairs, looking out the window, the divorce papers unfolded on the table beside him.

Shit.

Harper had the pocketknife out and he was running his thumb back and forth over the blade.

Cat padded to the chair opposite him and folded herself into it but didn't say anything. The sound of her heartbeat seemed to pound through the silence and she wondered if he could hear it as clearly as she did.

"When you said this was the last try," he said finally, "I guess it didn't really sink in. I mean, you've always been there for me. I can't imagine a life without you in it."

"I haven't been in it for a year and a half. Time may

have stopped for you, but it didn't for us."

Harper grimaced and leaned forward to brace his elbows on his knees, rubbing his face. Cat knew this was a shock, but it was one he needed. She hadn't planned on showing him the papers unless things fell through, but now that he had she would see where the conversation took them.

"Are you set on this?" he asked finally.

Wincing, Cat shook her head. "Definitely not. But if I had shown up at that hospital room and you had tried to shut me down I would have made you sign them. Yes, I would have been one of those women I despised, serving her man divorce papers in the hospital. Women like that disgust me, but I can kind of understand why they do it. It seems like I only ever see you in the hospital after you've been injured.

"But things haven't gone that way," she continued, "and I've actually begun to hope a little that at the end of this two weeks we might be able to go home together. Am I wrong in thinking that?"

She held her breath as she let him digest that last. But he didn't look up or say a word. The ridges of his thumb grated over the blade and every second that went by her hopes plummeted. After a solid minute she got up and walked out of the room before her bitter tears overflowed.

HARPER LOOKED UP as Cat left and almost called her back, but he needed some space. He had known she was waiting for him to respond about going home with her, but he just couldn't.

Maybe the divorce would be the best thing for all of them.

The thought of losing his family gutted him. They were his everything. He'd left *because* they meant the world to him.

Had he changed? Yes. Even he could see he wasn't as paranoid as he used to be. A lot of that was thanks to the counselor, but the space from Cat and the kids had helped too, whether she wanted to admit it or not.

The thought of trying to go back into a house with all of them gave him cold sweats. But it also sent a thrill of excitement through him too. He had missed his kids terribly. So much so that Cat wanting him to come home didn't freak him out as much as it used to. Harper had gone to Dr. Singh for months and he felt like he'd made a lot of progress with his paranoia, but how did he know for sure? What if he got into the house and they over-whelmed him again?

There would have to be limits and places he could retreat to be alone.

Damn. I'm actually considering this.

When he'd walked out the door in Virginia, he didn't know if he would be able to go back. And he still didn't now.

Maybe they could all start fresh in Colorado. But was it fair to the kids to pull them away from the life they knew?

He just didn't know.

God, there was so much going on in his freaking life right now he didn't know what to deal with first. Actually, he'd better go find Cat. He couldn't let her think that their growing closeness didn't mean anything to him.

Pushing up from the chair he went into the kitchen then down the hallway to her bedroom. Knocking on the door he pushed it open, but she wasn't there. She hadn't been on the deck. The last place he could think to look was downstairs.

The finished basement had a whole other kitchen/dining room/bedroom setup, as well as a pool table and a flat screen TV with a couple of video game consoles. Harper had checked it out that first day but hadn't been down since. It was nice and dim, though and his eyes eased almost immediately.

Cat sat in a rocking recliner, her foot pushing the chair into motion steadily. She looked up when he came down the stairs but didn't say anything. Harper felt like a royal ass when he saw her tear-stained cheeks and the tissues clutched in her hand. Cat was a strong woman. It took a lot to see her cry. The fact that she was crying now made him feel like the lowest kind of scum.

Crossing the room, he knelt down in front of her, stopping the chair. "I'm sorry I didn't respond to you. I'm kind of in shock. When I fell in love with you I just always thought it was forever. Even though my lifestyle didn't create stability, you did, Cat. You were always my stability. Walking away was the hardest thing I ever had to do. But I did it in the hopes that I could make myself better. It's not like a damned driving test where if I mark a wrong answer I get to take the test over again. I'm a trained killer. If I had screwed up in our house you or the kids were going to pay for it, possibly with your lives. I couldn't chance that."

Fresh tears rolled down her face and her expression crumpled. "I know. I knew that was why you left. Or at least that was what I had hoped. But it's been eighteen damn months—a year and a half—with you not letting us have any contact. If you had talked to us, or wrote…just something to let us know that we weren't all alone."

Cat sobbed and it broke his heart. Pulling her into his arms then down onto his lap, he held her as she let all her emotions out. Tears choked his own throat as he cradled her to him. "If I had called I would not have been able to stay away."

And that was the gist of his angst. God, yes, he wanted to be with them, but he was willing to give up his own happiness if it kept them safe.

Cat's arms wrapped around his neck and she looked up at him. "I have always had more faith in you than you have yourself. Always."

Nuzzling his face into her damp hair, he nodded. "I know that. Without a doubt. And whether you were with me or not your faith kept me going." Relaxing into his hold, Cat's tears began to slow. "I love you, Cat."

Her arms tightened around his neck till he thought something was going to pop.

"I love you too, damn it." Pulling back she cupped his face, looked him in the eye and gave him a glorious kiss.

Something in Harper settled square. It was as if his chassis had been running crooked, a little out of alignment. Cat made him feel like he was running true again. Maybe with her at his side he could get back where they used to be in their relationship.

The emotion between them changed easily to desire and within seconds Cat had stripped off her t-shirt to his avid gaze. Harper paused long enough to tweak her nipples, loving the instant reaction.

They loved like they used to, when their love had been strongest, getting lost in the feel of each other's bodies. As Cat rode him to completion, Harper was suddenly struck with the knowledge that he would do anything to stay with her.

Anything.

THEY SHIFTED INTO a new gear in their relationship. There were still a lot of things up in the air that they didn't know how to deal with yet, but they'd reestablished their love, the most important part of the equation. That night he moved into her bedroom. Cat mentioned at breakfast the next day that maybe they should bring the kids out.

That sent him into a bit of a funk again but Harper knew she was right. And maybe this was the best place to do it, neutral ground, where there were no guns within reach. His little pocketknife had sufficed for the few stressful times he'd had. Would it be too much to hope that he could put the guns away permanently around the kids?

When he told Cat he thought bringing the kids out would be a good idea the joy on her face made his torment fade. Harper knew she'd been talking to the kids every night and he wondered what she had told them about him.

"I told them you had been injured and were recuperating," she told him when he dared to ask. "No more than that."

Somehow that didn't make him feel much better about the situation.

Cat called to make arrangements to fly the kids out. Her mother would get them on the plane in Virginia and Cat and Harper would pick them up. They were scheduled to arrive in three days.

Harper suddenly felt like he was under the gun again. He called Dr. Singh and managed to catch her when she had some free time, so he talked with her for a while. When he hung up Harper had a better belief in himself that he could deal with whatever came up.

The day before the kids arrived they drove into Cañon City for a consult with a doctor recommended by the doctor from Amarillo. Harper's skin had been itching around his eye and Dr. Fleck agreed that the stitches could come out of the sensitive area. Cat held his hand as each little filament was snipped, then tugged free. Dr. Fleck also removed all of the stitches from his chest wound. "It looks good, it looks good. Whoever did the initial surgery on it did an excellent job. You won't have much of a scar here at all."

Cat gave him a funny look. "Do you see a lot of gun-shot wounds in here, Dr. Fleck?"

The gray haired man laughed and bumped his glasses up the bridge of his nose. "You'd be surprised, young lady. Aftercare, yes. We're surrounded by several correctional institutions, both federal and state. Don't know if you've seen the signs warning you against picking up hitchhikers, but that's why. We actually have a pretty good trauma center too, because we get a lot of fighting injuries, knife injuries, that type of thing. Your husband isn't the first gunshot wound I've seen this year."

Cat's gaze connected to Harper's, as if she knew he would not like the idea of prisons around them. She had seen the one on 50 on the way into town, but hadn't thought much about it. Harper fought to keep his gaze steady and not reveal anything, but she was right to be worried. The thought of that many criminals around them made his protective instincts surge.

The doctor held up a hand mirror for Harper to look into and even he had to admit he didn't look too bad. The skin around his right eye was pink and tight and a little splotchy from the stitches being pulled. It was still bruised under his eye but he'd been injured enough though to know that it would heal up fine.

"And what about the eye itself?"

The doctor looked at him, considering. "Well, you've gone this long without getting an infection, so that's excellent. It looks like your injury was almost surgical in nature. A piece of shrapnel basically sliced through your cornea and the tissue around it. But if it doesn't get infected, nothing may happen. Your eye still has all of the blood flow it needs so you may just heal like this, with two seemingly perfect eyes. It's possible nobody may know you ever had an issue with it."

Harper almost wished for the opposite. If he was going to lose his eye it needed to be a significant injury. Right now he just looked the same as he always did. It looked like he'd been in a bar fight and popped in the eye. Something so devastating to his life needed to leave serious scars.

They left the doctor's office a few minutes later. Harper still needed the sunglasses, but the first chance he got to go shopping he'd be getting a set of Oakleys or something. The grandpa look had to go.

The doctor had given him one piece of incredible news.

Harper held his hand out for the keys and Cat tossed them to him with a grin. "No tickets," she admonished.

They tooled around town, just exploring. It was nice being out of the house and for the first time Harper felt like he was back on the road to normality. But then he looked over at Cat. Air blew in from the passenger side window, lowered just a bit to let in the spring breeze. Her dark hair flew in the light wind and she pushed it back with her lean fingers. She was a gorgeous woman and he would love to get his life back on track with her and the kids.

They went back to the house and parked in the garage. Circling the hood, he pulled Cat's door open and carried her into the house. As he dropped her to the bed in the bedroom, she laughed up at him. "Oh, really?"

He nodded once. "Yes, oh really. Get rid of those pants."

Without the fear of pulling stitches or lingering infection, Harper felt like a completely different man. It was all psychological of course, but the change was significant. It released a ball of tension he had been carrying around for too long. That release made him almost giddy and Cat caught onto his playful mood.

He nibbled his way up her long legs, pausing only long enough to tug her panties away before spreading her knees wide. Cat's breath caught as he kissed his way to the thatch of dark curls at the juncture of her thighs, then deeper. Sighing in pleasure she rested her hands on his head, giving him subtle directions. Her thighs tightened around his head as his tongue swirled around her clit, but he didn't let her dislodge him. Reaching up, he burrowed his hand beneath her shirt and bra, cupping her breasts. "Ah," she sighed, abdominals contracting as she rocked harder into his intimate kiss.

Harper relished feeling almost as vital as before he was wounded. The past two weeks had been a devastating blow, but now it was time to re-engage in life.

Cat rocked harder against his tongue and she began to gasp, twitching. Harper shifted, easing two fingers inside her slick channel. Cat groaned hard as he began to move his hand and within just a couple of minutes she climaxed. As Harper looked up the line of her undulating body and tasted her decadent release on his tongue, he thanked his stars that she had come to Amarillo for him.

Barely giving her time to catch her breath, Harper gripped her hips and flipped her over. Dragging a pillow from the head of the bed he wedged it beneath her hips. Crawling up her body, heavy thighs outside of hers, Harper fisted himself to guide into her. Cat arched up as he slid deep and began to move.

"Oh, yeah," she sighed, face turned to the side. "This is what I was waiting for."

Harper surged harder, trying to be gentle, but there was something compelling him to claim her. Cat was already his wife, technically, but he wanted to reestablish his place in her life. And today was the first day he almost felt like himself.

She arched her hips even more and something about the angle of his cock and that heavy vein gliding over her pubic bone sent him over the edge. With a shout Harper came, losing himself in the feel of her body undulating beneath his.

Panting, muscles quivering, he let himself drop to the mattress beside her. Cat panted as well, but her eyes glittered with satisfaction as she smiled at him. Harper grinned back but couldn't muster enough energy to do anything more than that. His eyes drifted shut and he didn't even notice when he drifted off to sleep.

CAT WATCHED HARPER'S face go slack.

Damn, he was gorgeous.

The skin around his right eye was a little inflamed,

with a couple specks of blood where the stitches had been removed, but it would heal. Considering he'd been at death's door a couple weeks ago he looked damn fine. His dark buzz cut needed a trim but she wasn't going to remind him—she liked it a little longer. Maybe if she asked nicely he would let it grow a little more.

The beard was thickening as well, softening. She hadn't even noticed it when he'd, well…her mind was on other things at the time.

Harper snuffled lightly in his sleep and she grinned at the sound. Definitely not that of a super-elite warrior.

He heaved out a breath, turning on his side. A frown crossed his face as though the movement pained him, then he relaxed again. The scars on his chest were more angry, flushed red. But they were like all the other injuries he'd gotten. They would fade with time.

She stretched, luxuriating in the aches from her body. For the first time in a long time she felt like part of a team again.

Cat slid out of bed and headed to the shower. There were things she needed to do before they left to pick up the kids tomorrow afternoon.

CHAPTER NINE

HARPER VACILLATED BETWEEN overjoyed to see his kids and terrified. And until they walked off the landing he didn't know how he was going to react.

Tate saw him first and bolted toward him, Iron Man backpack falling from his fingers to the concourse floor, gap-toothed grin wide. Harper leaned down and caught his son as he slammed into him, lifting him into his arms. Then Tate's strong little arms were unyielding in their strength as they wrapped around his neck. Harper absorbed the unbridled joy and returned it tenfold. "You've grown so much," he whispered, amazed at what a man his child was turning into.

Both kids were beautiful. Tate looked a little wild after sleeping on the plane. Dark hair stood on end and his fair skin was flushed, but his burnished golden eyes, the same as his mother, shone with happiness. Dillon had the dark hair but had inherited his own gray eyes. And right now they were as cold and unyielding as he knew his own could be.

The girl stood cradled in her mother's arms. There were tears in her wounded eyes but she refused to let them fall. Still carrying Tate Harper walked forward, one hand held out. But Dillon turned her face into Cat's chest.

He tried not to be hurt at the rebuff, but he was. And she had every right to treat him that way. Time after time he had let her down. Hell, if he boiled everything down he'd basically been a sperm donor. Other people had been there to welcome her into the world, cheer her on for all her milestones. As he thought about everything he had missed nausea turned his stomach. They may never be able to recover.

Tate finally released his neck but refused to let go of his hand. After collecting the bags they headed for the Yukon, Tate jabbering a mile a minute. It seemed to Tate that all was forgiven. Or forgotten. Dad was back and all was well again. But even his enthusiasm began to wane in the face of Dillon's icy reserve. At one point he leaned over, whispering to his sister. Harper glanced at them in the rearview mirror. Dillon shook her head, arms crossed over her narrow chest, then turned back to the window.

Harper had no idea what he needed to do. The only thing he did know was that it was going to take time.

Cat reached over to rest her hand on his thigh and he was struck with such a strong sense of nostalgia it almost made him wince. They had ridden together like this too many times to count. Without conscious thought he realized that everybody had taken the same seats they always did when they went somewhere as a family.

He had been the one to ruin it. If he had been better able to deal with the paranoia that had plagued him, if he had sought help sooner, things would definitely be different.

That guilt would be added to all the rest that he carried.

CAT TRIED DESPERATELY to defuse the situation between Harper and Dillon but her daughter was being obstinate. She wouldn't even look at her father.

Tate had ten million things to tell her about, from the rusted Matchbox car he found on the beach at Grandma's house to the teacher at school that supposedly didn't like him. "I'm sure you're wrong," Cat murmured. "Teachers have to like all kids. It's in the job description."

Tate gave her a squinty eyed look, trying to tell if she was lying or not, but Cat kept her face straight. Within a few seconds he was off on another tangent. Then he wanted food. Then he had to pee. At one point she looked over at Harper and laughed. Obviously he had forgotten what it was like to live with a little boy. He looked more tired than he had the past few days.

After a few stops and starts they made it down the road. They drove down the main strip of Cañon City.

"Mom, why do those signs say not to pick up hitchhikers?"

Cat glanced back at her daughter, debating what to tell her. "Well, there are a couple of prisons around here. There's a big one just outside of town we'll pass. They don't want people picking up criminals."

Even in the dimming evening light she could see Dillon's eyes go wide, then she turned to look back out the window. She was probably trying to decide which of the many pedestrians out right now were bad people. Tate didn't help matters when he pointed out a guy running across two lanes of traffic. "Oh, I bet he just robbed a store!"

Cat shook her head. "I think he's just trying to cross the road, kiddo. Like a bunch of other people do every day."

Tate looked a little disappointed but didn't contradict her. When she looked to Harper for a little parental solidarity though, it was to find his brows furrowed. His gaze scanned the area, head moving back and forth as if he were scanning for terrorists. Cat got a worried feeling in her chest and she reached over to rest her hand on his thigh. Harper jerked as if he had forgotten where he was.

"Are you okay?" she asked quietly.

He blinked, nodding. "Yeah. Lost myself a little there."

"I could see that."

He gave her a sheepish look. "I think I'm going to be hyper-aware now that the kids are here."

"I had a feeling you would be. And I don't mind it as long as it's within reason. I love you, Harper. We can deal with anything."

He stared at her for a long moment before jerking his attention back to the road. She thought she could see a shine of appreciation in his eyes though.

When they arrived at the house Tate was ready to explore but Cat put the kibosh on that. "We need to get you guys settled, then you need a bath before bed."

"Aw, Mom," he whined.

But she could see the tiredness in his eyes. Virginia was three hours ahead of Colorado so it was technically past their bedtime already. No, they didn't have school the next day but she wanted to keep them on the schedule they were used to.

And in spite of his protests, as soon as Tate's head hit the pillow his eyes began to droop. "I want Dad to tuck me in."

Harper was more than happy to accommodate him. Settling to the edge of the mattress, Cat watched him run his palm over Tate's dark hair. "You sleep good, buddy."

"I will. Love you, Dad. Glad you're back."

Then he burrowed his head into the pillow and was out.

Harper sat next to him for another minute and Cat rested her hand on his broad shoulder. He covered her hand with his own, then drew it to his mouth for a kiss. Holding on to her fingers he led her out of the room.

Dillon was in the den curled into the chair Harper normally sat in, ear buds plugged into her iPad as she swiped. She glanced up when they entered the room but didn't say anything, continuing to play. Or she at least pretended to. Cat noticed that her movements began to slow.

Cat and Harper sat on the couch and flicked on the TV. As Harper flipped channels she curled into his side, legs out beside her. She closed her eyes and rested her head in the crook of his arm. "I think I'm more tired now than I have been for the past two weeks."

His heavy chest rumbled under her ear as he laughed. "I have a new appreciation for what you've had to do while I was gone. The kid just doesn't stop."

"Until he gets tired. Then he crashes hard. Kind of like somebody else I know."

Harper was like that. He could stay up for days if he needed to, but as soon as his head hit the pillow he was out. He ran his hand up her arm. "I'm not like that anymore. I like my sleep."

Cat didn't contradict him outright, but she squinted up at him. They'd slept together the last few nights—he had actually moved his stuff into her room—and she knew he wasn't as sound a sleeper as he suggested. Several times she had woken up to find him gone. He came back toward morning, *then* he crashed. But she wasn't going to complain. They were on a much better track.

They watched a couple of semi-funny sitcoms. Cat was very aware when Dillon took out her ear buds and began to watch TV with them. But within a few minutes she claimed she was tired and headed to bed. Without a kiss or hug for either one of them, Dillon left the room.

Disappointment swelled but she forced it down. She couldn't expect the kids to welcome Harper within just a few hours.

Harper loved her a little more fervently that night, then cradled her in his arms. "How do I reach her?" he whispered.

Cat shook her head against him. "I'm not sure. It may take a while."

He heaved a sigh as if he had already assumed the answer.

As she was drifting off to sleep she felt Harper leave the bed to go do a check.

THE MORNING SUN had just cracked the horizon when Harper conceded he was tired. The worry about the safety of his kids weighed on his mind and he craved the feel of a rifle in his hands. No, not a rifle. His rifle. His security. Chad had taken the customized Barrett rifle back to Denver with him when Harper had been injured. Harper wanted to get his hands on the stock and scope to see how bad the damage was.

The kids' comments about the hitchhikers had roused his fighting instincts. He wanted to go out and slay every criminal in a fifty-mile radius whether they were a threat or not. Intellectually he knew the urge was unrealistic, but he still felt it. He settled for staying up and protecting his family through the night.

Heading toward the bedroom he stripped off his t-shirt. After a shower he'd hit the sack.

Dillon came down the hallway from her room and stopped dead when she saw him reaching for the door handle. Harper paused too, unsure of the reception he would get if he told her good morning. He was a little shocked when her mouth dropped open and tears filled her stormy eyes. Walking forward slowly, her eyes roved over his chest in horror.

"What happened?"

Harper swallowed, unsure what to tell his daughter. What had Cat told her?

"I was shot a couple of weeks ago."

Her eyes flashed to his as if to see if he were telling the truth. "Seriously?"

He nodded. "But I'm okay. No big deal," he assured her.

She shook her head, stepping closer. Her hand lifted as if she wanted to touch the wound but she stopped. "Does it still hurt?"

"Not much. I'm kind of used to it."

Crossing her arms, she looked up at him, considering. "Mom told me you had been hurt but she didn't say how or why. I thought she was lying to me again."

Harper winced. "She wasn't lying. I was shot in the chest and I was hit by glass when my scope was hit. I lost the vision in my right eye." He rubbed at the scars on his face a little self-consciously.

She blinked. "Isn't that your shooting eye?"

Harper looked at her, considering. Damn, she was sharp. "Yes, it is. I'm going to have to teach myself to shoot again. I don't really shoot much at work, but it's a skill I need to keep."

Dillon shook her head again, her expression forlorn. "Where do you work now? Mom didn't know. And we haven't heard from you in so long. It was like you disappeared off the earth. And now you're hurt." Tears filled her eyes again and one slipped down her cheek. She swiped it away angrily, but more began to follow.

"Oh, honey." Harper dared to take a step toward

her, heartened when she didn't bolt. "I'm okay. I really am. And I'm sorry I haven't talked to you. Believe it or not I've missed you too—I just didn't feel like I could be at home with you for a while. Not because of anything you did, but because of things that were going on in my head. I had to get them straightened out so that I could be with you guys."

Dillon didn't look like she believed him, but at least she was listening.

"I swear to you I wanted to come home, but I couldn't risk you guys. In my old job with the SEALs I had to go to war in bad places."

"Afghanistan?"

He stopped, surprised. But then, why was he surprised? Dillon was damn smart. "Yes. I was there for a good while. And a bunch of other places. And when you get used to doing something, like fighting in a war, it's hard to change when you come home. I had problems getting used to *not* fighting. Do you understand?"

She nodded, arms still wrapped around herself.

"So rather than run the chance of maybe waking up one night and hurting you guys I moved out. It wasn't because your mom and I had problems, it wasn't because I didn't love you and it definitely wasn't because of anything you kids did. It was just me. Fighting myself in my head. And I worried that if I talked to you guys I wouldn't be able to stay away."

Tears were still dripping down her cheeks. Harper dared to reach out and tuck a mussed strand of her dark hair behind her ear. "But I promise you I won't leave you again. Not like this. And I promise I will always talk to you. Okay?"

She nodded and took a step forward, as if seeking reassurance. Harper opened his arms for a hug and she folded into him, sobbing. "Oh, baby girl, I love you so much. I'm sorry I hurt you but I really did think it would be better if I just disappeared."

He ran his hands down her long hair and pressed a kiss to the top of her head. "Do you think you can forgive me? I really miss talking to you."

She nodded her head against him and wrapped her arms around him to squeeze, then pulled back with a gasp. "I didn't hurt you, did I?"

Harper smiled. "Nope. Not enough to notice."

He pulled her back for another hug and another kiss on top of her head. "Wanna grab some breakfast?"

Dillon nodded and they headed to the kitchen, his arm around her shoulders.

CAT WOKE TO giggles and a jiggling bed.

"Mom," Tate singsonged.

She cracked an eye open, smiling. "Hey, little man."

Then her eyes widened. Both kids and Harper were standing over her. They were all grinning and Harper held a wooden tray with food on it. Cat pushed herself upright in the bed, glad she'd slipped on a t-shirt at some point.

"What's going on?"

"We made you breakfast," Dillon told her.

Cat's brows lifted in surprise. "Really?"

The more amazing thing was that Dillon was grinning up at Harper like she used to. Cat met Harper's gaze and he gave her a little nod. Huh. There was a story there she'd have to get later.

Cat dug into her dubious breakfast but loved every minute of it because her family surrounded her, looking on with fun and enjoyment. For a moment her eyes filled with tears as she looked at their dear faces. "I love all you guys," she told them softly. Harper leaned forward, pressing a kiss to her lips.

"Hey, Mom? If you love me can I have your last piece of bacon?"

She pulled back, laughing. "Yes, my little dispose-all, you can have my last piece of bacon."

CAT MADE A concerted effort to keep Tate busy while Harper and Dillon got reacquainted. When the kids left to clean up the breakfast dishes he whispered to her about the incident earlier that morning. Her eyes had filled with tears. Dillon needed her father and vice versa. They were so similar it was eerie at times.

As they began to leave the yard on a hike a few hours later, Harper glanced back at her. Cat waved to affirm she'd seen what he was doing and went back to Tate.

When Harper and Dillon returned it was obvious they had talked a lot. The tension that used to stretch between them was completely gone. Dillon hung on her father like she'd used to.

When Harper suggested they head in town for an early dinner she looked at him in surprise. "Are you sure?"

Nodding firmly, he tilted his head toward the kids. "It's one thing for me to hang around like an invalid but they need to run. We'll just go in for dinner. Maybe bum around a bit."

Cat thought it was a cool idea so she left to clean up. Harper wouldn't have suggested it if he didn't feel ready, right?

They turned on SR 50 when they left the house and Cat was struck by the beauty of the unforgiving landscape. It was a little hypnotizing. After a few miles they rounded a bend and came upon the huge prison.

"Wow," Tate gasped. "What's that place?"

"It's a great big place to keep bad people."

Tate's eyes widened. "Really?" He craned his neck as it slid behind them.

Cat motioned to the left. "If you turn here you can see the old prison. I remember catching a glimpse of it when we came through town a few days ago."

The coasted past the old building with the huge guard tower at the corner.

"Can we go inside?" Tate asked.

Cat frowned. "I think they have tours but I'm not sure we want to spend the last of our time there. Besides, I think it's too late tonight."

Once they arrived in downtown Cañon City Cat was delighted by little artist shops scattered here and there downtown.

Harper must have seen the enjoyment on her face because he pulled over into an empty parking spot. Cat grabbed her cell phone from the charger and leaned over for a quick kiss, then slid out of the truck. "I'll be right in here in this downtown stretch." She indicated the area where they were, populated with unique little art stores.

Dillon unsnapped her seat belt. "Can I go with you, Mom?"

Cat nodded and waited while the girl hopped down out of the truck.

"We're going to go get gas," Harper told her, "and see what there is for us men to do."

Tate grinned at being included in 'men' and Cat laughed. "Okay. There was a Sears on the other end of town. I think we'll be here for a while but if we move I'll let you know."

Cat and Dillon wandered through shop after shop of beautiful handmade artwork. There were pottery shops, leather shops and others that kept a little bit of everything. Her creative side luxuriated in all of the brilliant ideas and colors.

Dillon seemed to enjoy the outing as well. Cat bought her a set of watercolor pencils, explaining how they were used to create the stunning paintings on the walls. She seemed intrigued and happy.

One shop they wandered into held bone-handled knives.

"Do you think Dad would like one of these?"

Cat looked at them in consideration. Though Harper usually carried a different style, she thought he would enjoy something unique.

"I like that one." Dillon pointed to a blade set on a little stand. "Why does it look like that though?"

"That's a Damascus blade. It's a way of treating the metal and it's extremely strong," Cat told her. "Kinda looks like flowing water on the blade, huh?"

The clerk, obviously sensing a sale, pulled the blade from the display case and held it out to Cat. "You are absolutely right, ma'am. This is a Damascus steel blade made by a local artisan, a Master Smith in blade making. Be careful. It is very sharp."

Cat took the knife and tested the fit in her hand. It was too big for her, but it would fit Harper's grip perfectly. The blade was straight and strong. When the clerk took it back he showed her how sharp it was by skimming a piece of paper over the edge. It split into two halves immediately.

She had to admit she was impressed. "Maybe this could be a late Christmas present?"

Dillon nodded, wide eyed. "He would love it. He would appreciate that the guy that made it is a Master."

Cat grinned, wondering if Dillon even realized what that meant exactly. Though it was expensive, she nodded to the clerk to wrap it up. It also came with a handmade leather sheath by another local artist.

They were grinning when they left the store, the knife securely wrapped and snugged in her purse. Cat refused to think about the money she had just spent. It would be worth it just for the expression on Harper's face. They could give it to him over dinner.

Holidays had always been difficult because they never knew if he was going to be home or not. Over the years Cat had bought many Christmas and birthday presents that were never gifted on time. He would get them eventually. She had a boxful at home now, just waiting to be unwrapped. It was another little disappointing tradition she would like to be done with.

The thought of waking up and seeing his face every day was unfathomable to her. For so many years they had been ships passing in the night, sometimes literally. She could remember a couple of instances over the years when he would make it home then be called out again almost immediately. The government didn't care if they were in the middle of eating dinner or making love. They expected their men to come when called.

Chad and Duncan had seemed like much more understanding bosses. She knew Harper would be called away working for them sometimes, but surely not months at a time.

Cat paused on the sidewalk and stepped close to the wall to call Harper. They were at the end of a block trying to decide which way to go. Cañon City wasn't very big but she thought they had walked what they wanted to.

"Mom, I don't like the way that guy is watching us."

Cat looked at Dillon, then toward the nod of her head. A man sat on a bench across the street but he was looking at the phone in his hand.

"As soon as I said that he looked down," Dillon murmured.

Cat found Harper's number and dialed. When he picked up she had to stop and look at the phone for a second. This was the first time he'd actually answered the damn thing in months.

"Hey, we're at the corner of Seventh and Main. Can we arrange a pick-up?"

"Absolutely," he promised. "Give us a few minutes."

"Okay. We're going to start walking back toward the prison."

"I'll be there as quick as I can. I love you, Cat."

Tears started in her eyes and she could barely open her mouth to respond. "I love you too, Harper."

She shook her head and shoved her phone into her pocket. The entire call had been strange and nostalgic all at once. "Let's walk back toward the prison."

Dillon was looking the opposite direction, though. "Is that a pet store? Can we go in super quick?"

Cat looked across the intersection. There was indeed a pet store sign hanging above a store. "It's getting a little late. I don't think it's open."

"The light is on."

True. "Okay, but just for a minute. Your dad will be upset if he can't find us."

They jogged across the street and into the pet store. The older man was getting ready to close up but he smiled when they walked in and leaned the broom against the counter. Dillon listened, rapt, as he told her about the animals he had in his cages. Cat felt guilty taking up all his time then not taking one of the residents, so she bought a dog toy for Hooch before they left the store. "We need to start back."

The evening light had faded and now the street was mostly lit by streetlights and a couple of bars farther down. They crossed the intersection and were heading toward the prison when a man stepped out of a doorway, bumping into them. Cat felt the tug on her purse strap and jerked away. "What the hell do you think you're doing? Let go."

"I just need a little money." The guy had a hand on her bag, refusing to let go.

Cat jerked but the guy was strong. "Let go now!"

They tugged back and forth. Cat was extremely glad the purse she carried had a heavy-duty strap because there was no way she was letting go.

In the background Cat heard a slight bark of tires but she didn't dare hope it was help. "Dillon, run!"

Dillon didn't get a chance to. Cat heard thumping footsteps on the pavement as somebody pounded up behind her. The thief must have sensed he was in mortal danger because he suddenly released the strap. But he was too late. A massive shape flew by her and slammed the guy against the wall. Harper drew his massive fist back and let loose. She heard bones break and the man went down like a ton of bricks, out cold. Cat staggered but Harper caught her. He dragged her into his arms, squeezing. "Are you okay?"

Cat nodded, a little dazed. That had been the craziest sixty seconds of her life. She wasn't even sure it had been that long.

The guy moaned on the ground but didn't wake up.

Which was probably a good thing because Harper was ready to kill him. He took a step toward him, but Cat pulled him back into her arms. Tension thrummed through his heavy muscles.

They called the police and a cop arrived within a few minutes. Officer Green seemed young but competent as he took in the scene and recognized the man on the ground. Cat urged Dillon to get back in the truck with Tate as they dealt with the report.

"So you were playing tug of war with him?"

Cat nodded. "I had called Harper a few minutes ago to come get us, then we went to the pet shop. When we left the store we didn't see anyone, but he was hiding in that doorway." She made a motion with her hand to a shadowed area.

"How long did you wrestle with him?" the officer asked.

Cat shook her head. "I think it felt longer than it actually was. Maybe a minute."

Officer Green turned to Harper. "You arrived then, correct?"

Harper nodded.

"How many times did you hit him?"

"Once."

The officer frowned at the short answer, then looked Harper up and down. Cat knew she couldn't have withstood one of Harper's heavy fists. She doubted the officer could have either.

"Sounds pretty straightforward to me. In future though, if somebody tries to take your purse just let it go,

Mrs. Preston. You're lucky you didn't get hurt."

Fuck that. Harper's present was in that bag and there was no way she was going to lose it.

An ambulance had to be called because even a few minutes later the man still hadn't regained consciousness.

The ambulance arrived quickly and checked him out. "Well," the older paramedic told them, "he's definitely got a broken nose but I think you just rung his bell. He's high on something so that's helping to keep him under too. We'll transport him."

Officer Green gave them each a friendly look. "He'll be in jail for a while. We have a bench warrant out for his arrest too. Dan is one of those guys that gets released from prison then lingers. He's had a string of minor incidents but nothing like this. I'm just glad you weren't hurt, Mrs. Preston."

Cat nodded. "Me too. Thank you so much, Officer Green."

Cat and Harper were free to go. As they climbed into the Yukon they looked at each other in disbelief. "What the hell?" Cat murmured.

Shoving the truck into gear, Harper began to drive. "Let's get the hell out of here."

"Wait!" Dillon pointed down the street. "I called in pizza because I knew you two would want to go home. I hope that's okay?"

Cat could have kissed her daughter. If the truck had been any smaller she would have reached back and done exactly that. "I think pizza sounds perfect. Good job, Dillon. Great thinking."

Pizza Madness was only two blocks down and on the opposite side of the street. Harper went in to get it while the rest of them stayed in the truck. Cat was happy to let him do that. She honestly didn't feel like doing anything right then.

When the rear door started to open Cat jerked, but it was only Harper putting the pizza in the back. She looked down at the subtle trembling in her hands.

Harper climbed behind the wheel and must have realized she was a little shocky. He gripped her hands with his own. "Cat, you did fine. You did exactly what I would have done if I had been in your position. You held out until help could get there."

She nodded, wondering how the hell he'd known she'd been replaying the scene in her mind. "I'm so glad you got there when you did."

Cat wouldn't cry over the creep that had attacked her; she was better than that. But the relief she felt that Harper was close was significant. For the first time in their marriage *he* had come to *her* rescue.

Harper seemed to realize that as well. "It felt amazing being the one to save you, Cat. I can't remember ever doing that before."

As they left town, driving past the old and new prisons, he held her hand all the way home.

Cat brushed off the incident and they managed to have a fabulous night. After they ate pizza and were lounging on the couches in the den, Cat retrieved her battered purse.

With a laugh, she drew out the boxed item. "There

was a reason why I wouldn't let him have my purse. Yes, replacing my ID and bank cards would have been a pain in the ass, but he also would have gotten your late Christmas present."

Harper looked down at the wrapped box in his hands and for several seconds didn't say anything. When he looked up at her his expression was rueful. "You know, getting boxes from you overseas was the highlight of my deployment. Seriously. And even when I couldn't let you know I received them I always appreciated them. Thank you for that, Cat."

The kids went to their knees on the floor before him to watch the paper come off. When he lifted the lid from the box and pushed the tissue paper away he stared down at it for several long seconds. Then, pulling the sheathed knife out, he let the box fall to the floor.

Cat loved the reverence he used when he removed the knife from the sheath. "Wow," he whispered.

Harper loved the knife; she could tell before he even said anything.

"That's from the kids and me."

He looked up at her, his normally intimidating gaze softened with appreciation. "It is truly beautiful. Thank you."

Dillon then told him the background of the knife and that the artisan was local. Harper absorbed every detail, nodding when she pointed out details. Then he carefully sheathed the knife and pulled them all in for a hug. "You guys are amazing. Thank you. This is an excellent post-Christmas gift."

As they loved that night, Harper seemed especially solicitous of her. "If anything had happened to you I think I would have gone crazy. I love you, Cat."

"I love you too, Harper. And I can't tell you how happy I am that you came to my rescue."

Once again Harper took control of their lovemaking, sending her crying out to the heavens several times before he sought his own pleasure. And as he held her in the night Cat hoped that they would be this in sync always.

THE NEXT FEW days flew by. They hiked the mountain, played the video games and pool in the basement and basically relearned living together. Harper still got up every night to keep watch, new knife at his side, but she didn't get after him for it. She didn't want to rock the boat.

Dillon was the one that did that. "When are we going home?"

Cat looked at Harper. He'd just taken a huge bite of ham sandwich and he swallowed heavily. They had talked a little about the path their lives were going to take but they hadn't gotten down to specifics. They had had their heads in the sand, Cat supposed. It was just so perfect right now...

"Well," Harper said slowly, "I think we need to be a family again. I have a good job here. What do you guys think of moving to Colorado?"

Dillon's mouth dropped open in surprise. "We

wouldn't be going back to Virginia? What about Grandma and Grandpa?"

Cat sighed. She had known this was coming. That was probably why she had avoided bringing it up. "Virginia is a beautiful place, but your dad has a new job up here that he really loves. And he has to get back to it soon now that he's pretty much healed. And your grandparents like to travel. They would love to come see us in Colorado."

Both kids looked at her with frowns on their faces, trying to decide if she was telling the truth or not. Her parents had been around for all of their young lives. It would definitely be a transition.

"Just think about it guys. And if you have strong feelings about it we can talk."

They nodded and were subdued the rest of dinner. Cat felt bad, but they had to have known things were going to have to change. Even if Harper came back to Virginia with them it would be a shake-up.

Later that night as they got ready for bed, Harper stroked a hand down her back. "You know, we don't have to go back to Colorado."

Cat looked up at him in surprise. "Why do you say that? I thought you loved your job."

He winced and walked around the bed, shucking his clothes as he went. "I do, but you guys are more important to me. If I'm going to commit to being with you, it's going to be anywhere. I'll find a job doing something."

Cat shook her head. "I don't think that's a good idea.

You've built a life here with men you respect. I see how your face lights up when you talk about them. Do you think you would be able to find anything comparable anywhere else?"

He shrugged, dropping to the mattress. He leaned back against the headboard, feet stretched out in front of him. "I don't know. LNF is a unique set-up. Finding somebody willing to hire a half-blind, paranoid former sniper may be a little difficult."

Cat lifted a brow at the way he said that and he shrugged.

"I think," she told him slowly, "that we shouldn't rule anything out. I have to say I'm a little excited at the thought of moving north. As much as I appreciate the SEAL community in Virginia I feel like it's kind of done for us. I'm not saying you shouldn't get together with your old team sometime, but I feel like we're ready to move on. The kids are at a good age to adapt to anything we do. And my parents will just have to learn to travel more." She shrugged. "I can do my work anywhere."

Harper nodded and tugged her down to lie against him. "Okay. We'll start looking for a house, then."

The kids still dragged their feet a little, but Dillon brought up something that Cat hadn't even considered. They were sitting on the sofa watching a new Disney movie, Dillon curled into Cat's side. Tate was sprawled on the floor, chin in his hands.

"At least if we move they'll quit calling us liars."

Cat didn't think she'd heard right. She looked at her daughter sharply. "What do you mean they call you liars?"

Dillon seemed to sense she'd bumbled because she tried to backpedal. "Nothing, Mom."

Cat shifted her daughter to sit up. "No, explain that. Who calls you a liar?"

Dillon sighed, looking down at her hands. Harper paused the movie. "Just some of the kids at school. Dad's been gone so long that they think we made up reasons why he was gone, but there are a lot of other military kids there. They knew he wasn't on deployment or anything." She shrugged uncomfortably.

Cat swiped the angry tears from her eyes. Why hadn't she thought of that? "I'm sorry, honey. I should have known kids would be mean."

Harper moved from the recliner and knelt down in front of Dillon on the couch. "I never meant to cause you so much grief, honey. I really didn't." He rested his big hand on her folded knee.

Dillon shrugged. "It's no big deal. It doesn't matter now that you're back. They can believe whatever they want."

Cat could tell that it had bugged Dillon though.

CHAPTER TEN

AND IT BUGGED Harper. Even hours later after everyone had gone to sleep he sprawled on the bed, arm folded under his head. "Maybe I should go to her school," he murmured, rocking his head to look at her.

Cat appreciated that he wanted to make things better for her. "That's very fatherly of you. But if we move it won't matter."

"Yeah, I guess you're right."

She ran her hand up the tight muscles of his arm. "I'm usually right."

Harper rocked his head toward her and gave her a narrow-eyed look, then rolled his whole body to loom over top of her. "You know," he said softly, "you are right most of the time. I have to admit that. I just hope you're right about us being together in a home again. I'm worried. For months I blocked myself off from that hope, but it's creeping in again."

Wrapping her arms around him, she leaned up to press a kiss to his chin. When he'd taken a shower earlier he'd shaved again. He knew she loved the feel of his smooth skin over his strong jaw, especially while kissing. "Then let it creep in. I'll fight for that hope. And the kids will too. You know that. These past couple days have been blissful for me because we're all finally together. You are the final piece to our puzzle."

She pressed her lips to his, trying to convey how much she needed him. They'd made love at least every night since they'd started, if not more, but it was never enough. Sometimes she would catch him looking at her like this was all a dream. Like she would disappear if he reached out to touch her. In those instances *she* reached out for *him*.

When he came to her with need and determination in his eyes, she welcomed him with open arms. He needed to believe that she would always be here for him.

As he stripped her nightshirt from her body, kissing every inch of skin he exposed, she cradled him to her. But she needed to convey something to him tonight.

Cat pushed up on his shoulders and slid out from beneath him. She dropped her panties to the floor then crawled back toward him across the mattress. As his gaze focused on her swaying breasts they both smiled because the effect on his body was instantaneous. Cat kissed her way up his thighs and around the growing bulge in his underwear. Moving deliberately she straddled his hips and leaned over him, her gaze connecting to his. Slowly she lowered herself to kiss his right eye, then did little nibbling kisses across the few fading scars there. "I love you, Harper."

His hands reached up but he only cupped her hips, letting her continue on her journey. She pressed a kiss to the scar across his right deltoid, an old injury from one of his first deployments, then his left collarbone, broken on a training trip to California. Then, moving carefully, she pressed kisses to the new scar still healing on his chest. That one had been too close to taking his life. Thank goodness he had been able to receive medical care as quickly as he did.

Cat moved down Harper's muscled abs and the slim line of black hair there. "I think everything about you is beautiful."

He puffed out a little laugh but she looked up at him with reproach. "I do. Your body is superb, even wounded. It always has been. That's why I always have to beat the nurses off you." She flashed him a grin. "Your mind is devious and brilliant, but I love that. The loyalty to your family and your men is humbling." She stroked a finger over the tattoo that echoed those sentiments on his right pectoral. "Your unfailing courage in the face of everything that has happened is astounding. I know whatever we have to face you will conquer with that same indomitable, dogged, Navy SEAL will. And your heart," she moved back up his chest to press a kiss to his sternum, "your heart is more loving and willing to try than I ever could have hoped. We're going to put our family back together," she promised.

Harper stared up at her for several long seconds before he closed his eyes, but not before she'd seen the shine of moisture in their depths. He pulled her down on top of him, burying his face into her neck. "You are every bit the woman you've always been, calm and understanding, willing to put up with my shit. And I have to tell you. All of those things you see in me? I wouldn't be any of them without you. And I mean that. You've supported me through everything. You flew across the country to be at my bedside even though you didn't know the kind of reaction you'd receive. It amazes me that you would take that chance. But I'm so glad you did. I love you, Catherine Marie Preston. I always have."

She flashed a smile at the use of her full name. "And I love you, Harper Broderick Preston. I always will."

They kissed like they always did, as if they were twenty-two again and had just fallen in love. Cat loved it when he cupped her head and guided her mouth over his own. Reaching down, she shoved his underwear away and cupped him in her quivering hand.

When she positioned him beneath her and sank down the communion felt almost spiritual. With his words he had aroused her like nothing else could and she could feel her release dancing within reach.

Harper bent his knees behind her and gripped her hips in his massive hands. Cat watched his muscles bulge beneath her as he took control of their movements. She had never seen a more glorious man.

Harper's face grew lax as he lost himself to the drives of her body flexing over his. One of his hands left her hips to cup her breast, tweaking the nipple. Cat moaned, wondering how long she could hold out. That sharp edge of tingling heat continued to build.

Harper began to pant. Cat knew that he loved the look of her body over top of his own. She leaned forward, her breasts bouncing a few inches from his face as he began to piston into her hard from beneath. That delight, the need she saw etched into his face had to echo her own.

And because they were in such synchronicity when he began to orgasm she did as well. Sublime pleasure arched her body over top of his and, unable to help herself, she sobbed. The release was emotional as well as physical and she would always cherish this night.

And as many more as they had ahead of them.

THOUGH SHE HAD paid for two weeks in the rental house, they completely scrapped all previous plans and left two days early to head to Denver. At the end of the weekend she and the kids would fly back home and wait for Harper to find them a house. The kids had a month and a half left of school before they were out for summer break. The situation wasn't ideal but she didn't think there was any easier way to do it. Moving across country with two kids, a dog and a household was going to be a pain in the ass no matter how she did it.

Harper dismantled all his little cameras and doodads, re-boxing them to take back to his boss. Cat packed the truck, suddenly struck with nervousness.

They were about to completely flip their lives on end on the mere hope that they could be together as a family again. Her parents were not going to be overjoyed.

Just then Harper walked out of the house. His straight dark hair was almost an inch long now, but it looked really good on him. For years it had never been much longer than a half inch. The granny shades had been retired, replaced with a reflective set of wraparound Oakleys. When he had those glasses on you couldn't even see the scars. That sharp jaw had been shaved clean, just like she liked it.

His body was well on the mend. Every once in a while she caught him wincing as he reached for something, but those times were fewer and farther between. As he hefted his duffle into the back of the truck her eyes traced down his magnificent body. The new blue jeans cupped his ass to perfection and the knife she had given him was snugged into the corner of his pocket. The Damascus blade had been packed away with care. The black Henley shirt he had stretched on over his massive chest and taut abs made his eyes look even more silver. He considered the color tactical but she just considered it sexy.

When he looked up at her and graced her with one of his rare smiles she couldn't help but return it. Yes, she had hope. More than enough for all of them.

HARPER WAS ATTACKED with nerves as he pulled into the parking lot for LNF a few hours later. Duncan would be in his office, he knew. Seemed like the man never left it. There was something inside of him urging him to claim his family in front of one of the best buddies he'd ever had. Duncan had been his original friend out here and it was only proper that he introduce them first. Yes, he'd met Cat at the hospital, but Harper didn't know if he was even aware of the kids.

"Are you okay?"

Cat's hand on his back and her question brought him back to the present. He'd already parked but he didn't remember doing it. He lifted his glasses and rubbed his eyes, blinked at her and realized the kids were watching him too. "Yeah, I'm good. Just…this situation is a little surreal. I honestly never thought you would ever be a part of my life up here. These men have become my family and a few of them have started their own families. That made me miss you guys even more."

"Well, now Dad, you can have us all." Tate's matter-of-fact little voice said from the back seat.

Harper looked at him over his shoulder. "Yep. Looks that way, huh? Let's go."

He slipped his glasses on and stepped out of the truck.

To say that Shannon was surprised to see him, family in tow, was an understatement. Harper introduced her and the women shook hands, sharing smiles.

"Is Duncan in?"

Shannon nodded, looking dazed. "Of course. I think you can go right in. He'll appreciate the surprise."

Harper knocked and pushed the door open before he'd even heard a response, his hand firmly wrapped around Cat's. Duncan looked up and smiled in genuine pleasure, rocking back in his chair.

"Well, look what the cat dragged in," he drawled, running his gaze up and down.

Harper snorted at the joke the two of them had *never*

heard before. Cat laughed more appreciatively.

But Duncan's attention had been caught by the kids coming in behind them.

"Duncan, you know Cat, but these are my kids, Dillon," he rested a hand on her shoulder, "and Tate."

Harper lifted the boy up into his arms.

Duncan pushed up out of the chair and circled the desk, his face creased in a smile. He shook each of the kids' hands. "It's a true pleasure to meet you. Your dad is really something."

Harper caught the narrow-eyed look Duncan threw at him and he knew there would be questions later, but that would be all right. He could deal with questions.

"Hold on a minute. We just had a meeting." Duncan made a call and men began filtering in. Tate's eyes widened as Palmer rolled in, then widened even more when Flynn came in with Maya. The boy wandered over and immediately struck up a conversation with the wagging dog.

Harper shook Palmer's gloved hand. "'Bout damn time you got back," the third partner of LNF groused.

"Sorry I got shot, boss man."

Palmer waved the statement away.

Flynn held out his hand to Harper. "Good to see you, Preston."

Harper shook and nodded to the dog. "Tate's not going to bother the dog, is he?"

Flynn shook his head. "Nah. She'll take all the attention she can get." He moved aside as more men moved in to welcome Harper back.

Cᴀᴛ ᴡᴀᴛᴄʜᴇᴅ ᴛʜᴇ reserved look on Harper's face ease as one after another men entered the room, as well as a few women, to welcome him back. She was a little curious because he left his Oakleys on, but as she looked at the group she realized he wasn't the only one.

He turned to her suddenly. "Guys, this is my wife Cat, and my kids Dillon and Tate."

Fresh hellos circled the room and Cat could understand why he'd wanted to come back here. Yes, he'd had camaraderie in the Teams, but after he'd been injured the interactions had become stilted. As she looked around the room she realized Harper was one of the least injured men here, even after his recent injury.

"Where'd you get hit, big man?" A tall black man with a prosthetic arm leaned in, looking him up and down.

Harper pulled the V of the Henley over and down far enough that they could see the pink scar on his pectoral muscle. There were a few appreciative whistles but one guy, Brian she thought his name was, leaned in and scoffed. "Oh, whatever. I think Flynn's got you beat for gunshot wounds. Zeke's definitely got you beat for all other scars. You've been milking it the past few weeks."

They all laughed and that set the tone for the rest of their time at the office. The guys would come in and joke with him, but underneath it all she could see a visceral understanding. Even when their voices got quiet and he told them about losing his vision, lifting his glasses, there was still an empathy running through them all.

"Aren't they amazing?"

Cat looked down at the woman beside her. "Shannon, right?"

The woman nodded, smiling sweetly. "I've watched these guys for a couple years now and yes, they all get down, but as soon as they get together it goes like this. Upbeat, playing around, but with an understanding you could not believe. I'm so impressed that you're Preston's wife. How long have you guys been married?"

"Fourteen years. Dillon is twelve and Tate is six."

Shannon's eyes followed the kids as they played on the floor with the dog. "Wow. I'm so tickled there's another woman around. Preston is one of those scary guys that you're not really sure what he needs or even wants because he so rarely talks, but as soon as I saw the two of you together you made sense."

Cat smiled, touched by the sweet sentiment. "Thank you."

Chad entered just then and the already jubilant group laughed even more. As she watched Harper's smile spread at the gentle teasing directed his way she knew she would do everything in their power to secure a life here.

He looked up just then, searching for her. Cat gave a little wave and tipped her head at him, as if motioning him back to play with the other boys. Grinning, Harper turned back to the conversation.

HARPER COULDN'T REMEMBER a time when he had felt more complete. As he looked at the men in front of him talking shit about what had gone down he wondered how he ever would have been able to leave. Glancing at Cat sitting on the couch with Shannon, he felt a little stupid not letting her into this life sooner.

Chad bumped into him. "Hey, come here a minute."

Harper followed him out of the office and down the hallway to the exercise room. The smell of good sweat greeted him and his body yearned for a good workout. "I don't know if I can do a lot right now, Chad."

Chad shook his head, smiling, and motioned across the room. Harper glanced across and his gaze immediately focused on his weapon, positioned on top of one of the two-door cabinets that housed their miscellaneous gear. Without a word he crossed the room and lifted it down.

Removing his wrap-around Oakleys he set the rifle on the table, then sat in the chair before it. For a long time he just looked at the mess. A lot of time and money had gone into the customized Barrett MRAD .338 Lapua but Harper realized, looking at the destruction, that the weapon had saved his life. The composite stock had changed the trajectory of the bullet when it struck. If the stock had been wood the bullet would have continued on an almost straight path through that wood. But because it hit the composite stock it angled sharply up, hitting and shattering the scope.

Yes, he'd lost the sight in his eye but it was better than a bullet to the face.

Chad rested a hand on his shoulder. "The scope is done for, but I think you can salvage the Barrett."

Harper nodded in agreement. "Thanks for getting this. I think I needed to see for myself how bad it was."

"No problem, buddy. It was the least I could do. Let me know when you want to go to the range. I'll go with you."

Harper gave him a tight smile.

When he walked back into Duncan's office carrying the weapon, Cat's eyes went to it. And though she hadn't been trained like he had, she could immediately see the damage that had been done and what could have happened. Her glossy eyes met his in complete understanding.

Harper hated to leave the office. Everybody had stuck around to be friendly but they needed to get going. The kids were getting tired and they needed to find a place to stay. He'd already decided that his apartment was off limits. Too many unsecured weapons to be safe around the kids.

They settled on a decent hotel with adjoining rooms. They would only be here two nights before Cat and the kids had to fly back to Virginia.

Harper sank down into the office chair at the desk while Cat kicked off her shoes and sank to the edge of the bed. The kids were watching TV in the other room.

"Thank you for meeting the crew," he told her.

Cat gave him a funny look. "Why wouldn't I meet

them?"

He shrugged. That was a good question. "You were very gracious and warm. And nonjudgmental. That's a big deal in our group."

Cat nodded, understanding what he meant. Some of the guys there were really chewed up. Zeke had shown up just before they left and her heart had ached for the guy. But being through that kind of ordeal just made them stronger men, she would hope at least. "Zeke has a girlfriend, right?"

Harper nodded. "Some of the guys hang out at a place called Frog Dog. Ember is the daughter of the owner. Zeke really digs her."

Cat grinned, sensing it was an understatement. Shannon, sweet as she was, loved talking about people in love. Cat had gotten the scoop on most of the guys that were involved.

Duncan wasn't though, which Cat thought was odd. As the leader of their rag-tag group he appeared to be the most level-headed, centered, but he had no home life. Shannon wanted to find someone for the founder of LNF but hadn't yet met the right woman.

"Do you guys always get along?"

Grinning, Harper shrugged. "There's friendly rivalry. We have Marines and SEALs working together. There's bound to be some dust-ups. They're all good-natured though."

Cat could imagine. When the guys from the Teams got together they could be rowdier than twice the number of kids. Men that lived their lives on an adrenaline edge needed excitement in their regular lives.

A yawn suddenly hit her and she glanced at the clock. It wasn't especially late but they had done a lot today. Walking through the connecting door she found both kids already asleep, though the TV continued to blare. Using the remote to turn the set off she managed to get their shoes off and blankets over top of them. Crossing back to her room she went in the bathroom to brush her teeth. When she returned to the bedroom, Harper was dropping his jeans to the floor.

Cat blinked, appreciating his cute butt, but was too tired to do more than that. He stopped in front of her on the way to the bathroom and dropped a kiss to her mouth. Cat wound her arms around his neck and let him support her. "I loved your group. They are exactly what you need."

Damn, he felt good. Hard muscles poured off the heat and her legs sagged. Without a word he swung her up into his arms and carried her to the bed. Within seconds of being tucked in Cat had fallen asleep.

HARPER HOPPED IN the shower and allowed himself to soak in the scalding water. When he left the bathroom Cat was sound asleep, hands stacked beneath her cheek. It was still early.

Harper knew sleep would not come for a while so he redressed and let himself out of the room. Hotels put him on edge. Too many hiding places and exits. If he could walk the perimeter he might feel a little better about his family's safety.

Though he didn't plan it he found himself down in the parking garage unlocking the rear hatch of the Yukon. Hoisting his butt up on the tailgate he pulled the rifle case toward him and popped the latches. He wouldn't get the gun out; he didn't need overweight hotel security guards trying to save the world by calling him in. But he needed to look at it again.

The night vision scope he'd spent several grand on was a piece of trash now. The front crystal was totally obliterated. That had been what had screwed his eye, those little tiny shards. Seemed ridiculous that something so small could have such devastating impact.

He was thankful it hadn't been more than that though.

When he returned to the room an hour later he felt like he could sleep. Tomorrow they were going to look at houses and neighborhoods. Then the following morning Cat and the kids had to fly back to Virginia. He refused to be saddened by that.

They would be back.

THEY HAD AN interesting day exploring the outskirts of Denver. Cat loved how vital the city felt, as if there were always something going on. They identified a couple of areas where they would think about having a house. It was kind of a given that Harper wanted to be out of the city. She did too and the kids needed decent schools, but any more than that she would leave up to him.

That night they ate dinner in, wanting to spend as much time as possible together before their early morning flight out. The four of them watched silly TV and played, savoring being a unit again.

When Harper tucked the kids in that night Tate cried. "I don't want to leave you. Why can't I stay?"

Cat's eyes filled with tears as she watched Harper brush his hand over Tate's dark hair. "Because, buddy, we don't have a house or anything yet. While you guys finish out school I'm going to find us a place to live. That'll take a while. You have to pack up all your stuff and help Mom out. She has a bunch of work to do too to get ready. I promise you that we will be together as soon as we possibly can. I'll talk to you as much as I can, okay?"

Tate nodded and seemed to calm.

Dillon didn't say anything, just hugged Harper for several long minutes around the neck before releasing him. But Cat could see the glisten of tears in her eyes. Harper pressed a kiss to her forehead before leaving the room.

"I haven't felt this gutted," he growled, "since the day I left Virginia. Those kids are killing me."

Cat opened her arms and he stepped into them, tucking his face into her neck. "I love you," she told him softly. "And I think this is good for everyone. We all had a chance to reconnect—now we'll let the connection mature and remind us that we have an amazing family. We'll be back together in no time."

He nodded, lifting her to carry her to bed. There was

an unquenchable fierceness to his loving that night and she stayed awake as long as she could to absorb all those emotions. They would have to last her for a while.

THEY PARTED WITH tears and love. And determination to keep the lines of communication open, no matter what.

As Cat pressed her mouth to his for a final kiss, and then another final kiss, she fought back tears. They wouldn't do any good and would probably make the kids more upset.

Harper's jaw was clamped tight and his sunglasses on to shield the emotion he was feeling. The public didn't need to know how hard he was fighting right now to keep it together. Cat knew, though. She'd been with him long enough to recognize the signs that he was fighting for control. So even though she wanted to stay to the absolute last second, for all of their sakes she forced her legs to move. "Come on, guys, we have to get through security."

Tate sniffed and wiped his arm on his sleeve but followed along. Dillon gave Harper a last squeeze then walked away as well. All three of them kept glancing back as they went through security, until they couldn't see him any longer.

THEY'D BEEN HOME a couple days when Cat called her

mom and told her what was going on.

Angie Morgan seemed shocked but Cat could hear her trying to be understanding and she appreciated the hell out of her mom for doing that.

"Why Colorado, though? That's so far away."

"That's where his job is, Mom, and we've been apart long enough."

She sighed. "This is so sudden, though."

Cat sighed as well. They'd been over this a couple times already. "Mom, if we're going to move it will be easiest over summer break. Then the kids can settle in and start fresh at the beginning of the new school year."

"I guess," she agreed. "At least Harper wasn't hurt more. It sounds like he was lucky."

Cat thought of the rifle. "Yes, he was definitely lucky."

And so was she for not losing him.

THIS SEPARATION HAD been so vastly different from the last. Harper called at least once a night just to talk to her and the kids. Sometimes he used the Facetime app to see her and watch her go about her daily life. Cat propped her phone on a stack of recipe books and they talked about their days while she cooked dinner for the kids. It wasn't romantic in any way but it ended up bringing them closer than they'd ever been before, because it exposed Harper to a lifestyle he'd not really seen before. Even after he'd gotten out of the hospital a couple years ago and been home for several months he had been too lost in his own issues to take much notice of what she did with the kids.

Harper was definitely keeping those lines open now.

After the kids had gone to bed one night he'd also confessed to going back to the counselor. Cat wanted to cry because he truly was doing everything in his power to get them back together.

At night he also whispered how much he missed her. And what he was going to do to her next time he had her in his arms.

Then one afternoon she went to answer a knock at the door. It was Harper.

Cat flung herself into his arms with a squeal. "What the hell are you doing here?"

He looked a little pale in the face so she tugged him into the house. Coming back here to his old stomping grounds had to be hard.

He didn't give her a chance to baby him though. Kicking the door shut with a heavy boot he picked her up in his arms, his mouth slamming into hers. Cat opened for him, more than ready for anything he had to give her. After a month of going without her body craved his.

Dropping her feet to the floor he ripped her jeans open and shoved them down her hips. Cat arched with need, loving the desperation she could feel in him. She peeled her shirt over her head, then her bra. Harper knelt in front of her to pull her jeans off her feet, first her right then her left, but paused when she stripped.

"You don't know how much I need you right now,"

he groaned, burying his face in her breasts. Capturing a nipple with his lips, he suckled hard.

Cat cupped his head to her, her knees threatening to buckle. He still had his shades on but rather than deter her it spiked her arousal. "I'm right there with you, babe."

Pushing to his feet, Harper opened his own fly, exposing his heavy erection. Cat wanted to drop to her knees and take him into her mouth but he didn't give her a chance. With two hands behind her thighs he lifted her up against the foyer wall. Cat flung her arms around his neck and her legs around his hips. The head of his cock prodded at her opening and she angled her hips to take him in as he lowered her down.

They both groaned at the breach but they couldn't stop. Harper braced his feet and slammed into her over and over again. Cat cried out, her lips searching for his. He gave her a single kiss, then ripped his mouth away to surge back into her. Cat arched, her release looming closer. "Oh shit," she moaned.

Harper clenched her butt in his hands. Cat knew there would be bruises later but the sharp desperation was exactly what she needed right then. Harper gave a lusty groan and began to lose his rhythm, but Cat had gotten what she needed. With those last few strokes her orgasm washed over her in a euphoric wave. Harper found his own release, knees giving out as the orgasm consumed him.

When Cat opened her eyes she had to chuckle. They were crammed against the floor and wall, panting and a little sweaty. But she was exhilarated. Her skin tingled and she still rippled with aftershocks. "Well," she murmured, "I didn't expect that when I opened the door."

Harper began to laugh and he hugged her to him. Then with a hand braced against the wall he lifted them to their feet.

Cat hated the feel of him slipping out of her but she found her feet. It was amazing how quickly she'd become addicted to him in Colorado. This past month without him had been hell.

Harper slipped his glasses off and dropped them to the entry table and for the first time she could see his eyes. They were creased with humor and appreciation. Gray irises looked clear and healthy. There were some scars but they weren't nearly as pink and angry looking as they had been. All of the bruises were gone. He looked damn good. She stroked her fingers over the skin. "Still hurt?"

He shook his head. "I still get headaches but not like I used to." He winked his right eye. "This one's still dead but every once in a while I think I see a flash of something."

Cat's brows lifted in surprise. "Really?"

"Yeah, but I don't think it's anything. I followed up with the doc we use at LNF and he didn't seem particularly interested. He said it happens sometime when a synapse connects unexpectedly, or some shit like that."

He tugged on her hand, leading her down the hallway. "Let's go wash up real quick. I have something I want to do."

THE CLASSROOM THEY stopped at was packed with yelling kids. It was the last day of school for Dillon and Cat had debating even sending them. There definitely wouldn't be learning going on today.

She was glad she had made them go now.

When Harper walked into the room in his black BDUs and army green T-shirt stretched taut over heavy muscles he drew every kid's gaze. Dillon's eyes went round and her mouth dropped open, but she jumped up with a squeal and ran into his open arms. Harper made a show of swinging her around in his arms before dropping her to her feet and pressing a kiss to her hair.

He looked over her head at all of the kids staring at them, making sure to connect with every gaze. "Get your stuff, honey. It's time to get out of here."

That sixty-second display put him firmly at the top of the most hero-worshipped list.

HARPER STAYED FOR three days, a long weekend. But he had more surprises in store for them.

On Saturday her parents arrived. "Hope this is okay, honey. Harper told us to pack a bag and get up here. You haven't dismantled the guest room yet, have you?"

Cat shook her head, a little dazed. "No, not yet."

Her mother hustled down the hallway. Her father leaned over to give her a peck on the cheek. "He sounds like his old self, doesn't he?"

She nodded her head at her father.

That weekend Harper did everything he could to assure them that he would be a man Cat could depend upon again. But it didn't even take half that long. By afternoon it was as if he had never left their lives.

Sunday, apparently, he had arranged a barbeque with the guys from his old team.

Katey arrived at noon, looking frazzled but beautiful in a gauzy dress. At six months along she had the natural inner beauty that came with pregnancy, but also the energy. She brought bags of food and supplies. Lucas, her husband, arrived an hour later, loaded down with enough beer to float a house.

Cat tried not to freak out. Her house was mostly packed. She and the kids had kept essentials out for themselves but not much more than that. There were still some chairs in the backyard but not as many as she thought they would need. Luckily, everyone that arrived appeared to have brought their own chairs, as well as a casserole.

Katey ran the party like a drill sergeant directing troops. Or Navy SEALs, as it were.

Harper greeted everyone as they arrived. As soon as he saw Lucas walking up the drive he drew him into a tight man-hug. They had worked together for years. When Harper had been injured in Afghanistan it had been Lucas hauling him out.

Cat had always had an appreciation for the stocky blond because he'd had the fortitude to make sure Harper survived. For that she would always be grateful to him. When she told him that one day he had shaken his head. His eyes had darkened and his carefree attitude had faltered. She could see the ghosts of memory in his eyes. "That man saved me and my men more times than we can ever count. We all owed him everything we could do to get him out."

She'd had to turn away then, too choked up to speak.

As she watched him with most of his team now he began to lose his stiffness. SEAL Team 8 consisted of mostly younger guys and whether he recognized it or not, they looked up to Harper. She didn't know if it was for his age or skill or experience, maybe all three, but there was definitely a deference there. For some reason though she didn't think it was because he'd been injured. Harper had told her he'd withdrawn from the team because they couldn't deal with his injuries but maybe it was because *he* was no longer comfortable being around them with his injuries.

They joked around now like they'd never parted. As the kids played in the back yard and friends surrounded them she had to breathe in the moment. They stood on the edge of a precipice, about to launch into a new life. But they were getting the closure they needed with the old life. And she had to credit Harper with all of it.

That night as she and Harper lay in bed talking about the night she told him how much she admired his courage in coming back. He cranked his head around and looked down at her, a heavy scowl on his face. "Whatever," he paused. "Okay, maybe I did have some things weighing on me that spurred me to come down this weekend. I couldn't let kids at school call my daughter a liar. That chafed like crazy. And I needed to tell the guys how much I appreciated them. I don't think I did that at all after I got hit. That was several years overdue."

Skimming his hand down her arm he laced his big fingers with hers. "And I needed to clear the air with your parents. I left you in a serious lurch when I took off and I wanted to make sure they knew I would never do that again."

She chuckled and poked him in the ribs. "Well, you better tell me too."

He blinked at her and she realized she'd shocked him. Immediately he sat up on the bed. "Fuck, Cat, I didn't think I needed to tell you. I'm so invested in you, in us being together again I can't think straight. Why do you think I came down here? Yes, I had loose ends but I also just plain wanted to see you again. When you walked in that hospital room door you started an irreversible chain of events. I would have come back eventually, somehow, but getting shot made you come to me sooner. I'm actually appreciative that I got wounded because I don't know when I would have taken the initiative to do anything about our situation. You forced me to see that we're better off together. I love you, damn it. How can I not be with you now?"

Tears rolled down her cheeks. Lifting her up in his arms he spread her thighs over his lap, cradling her to him. Then he looked down into her eyes. "You are the most amazing woman. You've put up with so much of my crap and I pray that you'll put up with a little more. I'm trying to do the best I can but it's a process, you know?"

She snorted and sniffed, nodding. Wrapping her arms around his neck she buried her face against him. "I love you, Harper. I would have waited for you, but it was getting so hard."

Fresh tears dripped from her jaw but he wiped them away and cupped her face to look at him.

"I know, babe, but you don't have to do it alone now. I promise you I will be here when you need me, any time. And I will never shut off communication like that again. Just write off that year and a half to me being a stupid, stubborn, idiotic man, okay?"

Sputtering, she rocked her head against him. "I will," she whispered.

"I love you, Cat. So very much."

"I love you too, you stubborn man."

They laughed and cried and fell into each other's arms.

EPILOGUE

HARPER HAD FOUND them a house outside of Denver. Isolated and loaded with mature pines, the log cabin and the property around it made her eyes water with its beauty. "This is ours?"

Harper nodded, stretching his arms above his head. They had just driven for two days straight. Harper drove the U-Haul and she drove her SUV. They were beyond ready to be done. The kids took off to claim rooms. Hooch, the mutt they'd adopted years ago, wandered off to find something to pee on.

"Yes. I assumed you'd like it. It has everything you wanted. Good schools for the kids, shopping within driving distance, an office space for you to disappear to and a kitchen large enough to feed an army. Or a SEAL," he told her with a grin.

He motioned with his hand to a building on the left. "It has a detached garage for me and a small shop where I can do gun work. Plus, there's a valley about half a mile away where I can train my weak eye."

She looked around, seeing what he envisioned. It all sounded perfect.

After his impromptu visit to Virginia he'd had to return to work for a few weeks. But as soon as he'd closed on the new house he'd returned to help her finish packing up their Virginia house. It was already listed with a realtor and would sell in no time because of its proximity to the schools and Norfolk.

She crossed her arms beneath her breasts and raised her face to the sky. She'd just travelled sixteen hundred miles in two days, but suddenly she felt more energized than she had in a long time. She slipped her arm through Harper's. "Show me my new house, babe."

THE END

If you would like to read about the 'combat modified' veterans of the **Lost and Found Investigative Service**, check out these books:

The Embattled Road (FREE prequel)
Embattled Hearts – Book 1
Embattled Minds – Book 2
Embattled Home – Book 3
Her Forever Hero – Grif
SEAL's Lost Dream – Flynn
Unbreakable SEAL – Max

OTHER BOOKS BY J.M. MADDEN

A Touch of Fae
Second Time Around
A Needful Heart
Wet Dream
Love on the Line Book 1
Love on the Line Book 2
The Awakening Society – FREE
Tempt Me
Urban Moon Anthology

If you'd like to connect with me on social media and keep updated on my releases, try these links:

Newsletter: jmmadden.com/newsletter.htm
Website: jmmadden.com
Facebook: facebook.com/jmmaddenauthor
Twitter: @authorjmmadden
Tsū: www.tsu.co/JMMadden

And of course you can always email me at authorjmmadden@gmail.com

ABOUT THE AUTHOR

NY Times and USA Today Bestselling author J.M. Madden writes compelling romances between 'combat modified' military men and the women who love them. J.M. Madden loves any and all good love stories, most particularly her own. She has two beautiful children and a husband who always keeps her on her toes.

J.M. was a Deputy Sheriff in Ohio for nine years, until hubby moved the clan to Kentucky. When not chasing the family around, she's at the computer, reading and writing, perfecting her craft. She occasionally takes breaks to feed her animal horde and is trying to control her office-supply addiction, but both tasks are uphill battles. Happily, she is writing full-time and always has several projects in the works. She also dearly loves to hear from readers! So, drop her a line. She'll respond.

Made in the USA
San Bernardino, CA
20 April 2015